'hey're still there,' breathed Frankie, pointing to
e pipe and tobacco tin on the mantlepiece.
   I've kept them in their place ever since that
ght,' said Grandma Elliott. She rose from the chair
1 reached out to touch the pipe. 'He was here,'
: said into the silence. 'Do you believe me now?'
   'Yes,' said Michael, and no one ocntradicted him.
   'He's warning us,' said Grandma Elliot. 'It's a
arning about Devil's Hole. You have to tell Trident
Oil to leave that place alone. Otherwise, I'm warning
ou, people will die.'

Ann Coburn

DARK WATER

RED FOX

The author graetfully acknowledges the assistance of the
Arts Council of England

A Red Fox Book

Published by Random House Children's Books
20 Vauxhall Bridge Road, London SW1V 2SA

A division of Random House UK Ltd
London Melbourne Sydney Auckland
Johannesburg and agencies throughout the world

1 3 5 7 9 10 8 6 4 2

First published in United Kingdom 1998
by The Bodley Head Children's Books

Red Fox edition 1999

Set in Janson Text by
Palimpset Book Production Limited,
Polmont, Stirlingshire

Printed and bound in Norway by
AIT Trondheim AS

Papers used by Random House UK Limited are natural, recyclable
products made from wood grown in sustainable forests.
The manufacturing processes conform to the environmental
regulations of the country of origin.

RANDOM HOUSE UK Limited Reg. No. 954009

ISBN 0 09 964331 6

For Amy, Ben and John

'The dragon-green, the luminous, the dark, the serpent-haunted sea . . .'

James Elroy-Flecker, 1884–1915

1

'She wants you.'

David stopped halfway up the gangplank and twisted round to peer over his shoulder. A small boy was standing on the quayside.

'Getting tired?' called Michael, appearing at the top of the gangplank.

'No way,' said David. He sprinted the rest of the way and dumped the box he was carrying into Michael's arms. 'I only stopped because that little kid down there yelled something.'

'She wants you,' piped the boy a second time.

David leaned against the handrail, pushing his fair hair back out of his eyes. Michael dropped the box and joined him. They stared down at the boy, both glad of an excuse to stop loading the supplies. It had turned into a competition, with David running up and down the gangplank and Michael sprinting between the boat's deck and the galley, each refusing to admit he needed a break.

'Who wants us?' asked David.

'Grandma,' said the boy.

Michael scanned the quayside. Alice was struggling towards the boat with another box of supplies from Mr Madigan's car and Ian Elliot was strolling away from the harbour master's hut with his charts rolled under his arm, but there was no sign of anyone else.

'Where is she?' asked Michael.

The boy waved vaguely at the cliff behind him.

'She's up a cliff?' said David.

Michael smiled. 'I think she must live in Fisherman's Row,' he said, pointing to a terrace of sturdy, low cottages set into the sloping cliff above the harbour. Fisherman's Row basked peacefully in the evening sun, but as Michael gazed at it an unaccountable chill made the hairs rise on the back of his neck. He shuddered and looked away.

'Why does your grandma want us?' asked David, speaking to the boy slowly and clearly.

'Not *my* grandma,' said the boy, looking at David as though he were stupid. 'Grandma Elliot!'

'Elliot?' panted Alice, arriving at the bottom of the gangplank and dropping her box. She pointed to Ian, coming up behind her. 'Is it Mr Elliot you're after? The pilot?'

'Hey, you guys!' yelled Frankie, appearing on deck with her dad behind her. 'We're waiting to stow those supplies. Stop shirking!'

'Mr Madigan, someone wants Ian,' said Michael, pointing to the boy.

The boy shook his head. 'Not just him. All of you.'

'But we're about to sail,' said David, and he grinned as a thrill of excitement ran through him at the thought of the voyage ahead. 'We're leaving any minute.'

'Grandma Elliot knows that,' said the boy.

'She would,' said Ian, strolling up to them. 'Grandma Elliot knows everything.'

'She says you're all to come,' said the boy. 'She says now.'

Michael looked over to the cottages, then down at Ian Elliot, willing him to say no. Ian shoved his hands into his pockets and shuffled his feet like a boy summoned to the head teacher's office.

'Tell her we'll be right up,' he muttered.

'Which cottage is hers?' asked Frankie, jogging beside Ian as he led the way along the quayside.

'The end one. See?'

'I see it,' said Alice. 'She must have a brilliant view of the harbour and the sea. Is she really your gran?'

Ian nodded and started to climb the steps from the harbour to the cottages. 'That's right. She's my dad's mum.'

'Boy, she must be ancient!' said Frankie.

'That's not a very nice thing to say,' said David. He glanced nervously at Ian, but the big man was laughing.

'Yes, Trouble. She is very old.'

'How old?' asked David.

'I don't know exactly,' Ian admitted. 'But she's definitely over eighty.'

'Did you hear that, kids?' panted Frankie's dad as they reached the top of the steps. 'Over eighty. We'll need to be quiet and make sure we don't tire her.'

Ian Elliot hooted with laughter. 'You won't tire

her. She's as strong as a horse. She can climb these steps without getting out of breath,' he added, prodding a finger at Mr Madigan's heaving chest. 'But there is one thing you should know. She's just about blind.'

'Can't she see anything?' asked Alice, cringing as she remembered her comment about the brilliant view from the cottage.

'Light and shade, that's all. So remember to say yes or no to her, instead of nodding or shaking your head, and if you move anything in the cottage, you must put it back exactly where it was. You don't need to shout at her, though. She's not deaf. She can hear a flower open, that one.'

'What does she want to see us for?' asked Michael, softly.

'Good question,' said Ian, glancing at Mr Madigan. 'Good question. You four run on ahead. John and I just need to go over a few work problems.'

The two men fell back, talking quietly. The children walked in silence along the lane that led to the row of cottages, each building up their own picture of Grandma Elliot. David imagined a tiny, bent old woman with cobwebby white hair. Frankie thought she would smell of mildew and boiled fish, like Mrs Hardy in the apartment next to theirs back in California. Alice saw a woman in black with a white stick and a tragic face, while Michael, who was still feeling a strange reluctance to go near the cottage, prepared himself to meet a witch.

Grandma Elliot turned out to be none of those things. When the children reached her cottage, the front door was open. They hesitated, looking back at Frankie's dad and Ian, but the two men still had their heads together, deep in conversation.

'You took your time,' boomed a voice from inside the cottage. 'Come in!'

Alice went first, into a sunny yellow kitchen which took up the whole of the front of the cottage. The others shuffled in behind her, Michael last. The room was empty.

'Hello?' called Alice.

'Coming!' announced the voice. A door at the back of the room opened and Grandma Elliot walked in. Michael peered at the doorway behind her. It was too dark too see anything but, just before she closed the door, he caught a hint of a smell which made him shudder again.

The other three were staring at Grandma Elliot. She was very tall and only slightly stooped. Her eyes were a dense, milky blue colour, like the inside of a shell. Over her nose and cheekbones, the skin stretched as thin as cling-film, yet it draped her cheeks and neck in heavy folds and creases. Her short hair was thick, shiny and –

'– still red . . . it's bright red,' whispered David, nudging Alice in the ribs.

'I dye it, silly,' said Grandma Elliot, drawing her eyebrows together in a scowl which turned her wrinkles into deep furrows.

'Sorry,' said David, remembering too late Ian's warning about her sharp hearing.

'Look! She scowls just like Ian,' giggled Frankie.

'Who's she, the cat's mother?'

5

'OK. So what do I call you, huh?' challenged Frankie.

A hint of a smile crossed the wrinkled face. 'You must be Frankie Madigan.'

Frankie nodded, then remembered to speak. 'Yeah, I am. How did you know?'

'Easy. Your American accent. You can call me Grandma Elliot, everyone else does. Ian has told me all about you four friends. Always together. Always up to something. Frankie, you're the wild one with clothes like a rainbow. Am I right?'

David sniggered, then regretted it as Grandma Elliot turned her sharp-boned face in his direction. 'And you must be David. The farm boy. Of the earth and down-to-earth, hmmm?'

'How . . . ?'

'Did I know? My red hair shocked you. That told me a lot.' She smiled at David. 'That leaves Alice. Tall, dark and beautiful. Don't blush. It's true.'

Alice gasped and put her hands to her red cheeks.

'And you must be Michael.'

Michael was still staring at the door that led to the back of the house. He gave a gasp of shock at the mention of his name and Grandma Elliot chuckled. 'Yes, you. The little one hovering on the threshold who hasn't said a word yet.'

'Are you showing off again, Gran?' said Ian, ducking under the door frame and into the cottage.

'She's amazing!' said Alice.

'Folk around here say she has second sight!' hissed Ian, dramatically. 'Me? I think she's just nosy.'

Grandma Elliot laughed and threw an accurate punch which Ian dodged smoothly.

'Gran? This is my good friend John Madigan,' he said.

Mr Madigan walked up and took her hand in both of his. 'I'm very pleased to meet you.'

Grandma Elliot gave a sad smile and patted Mr Madigan's hand. 'You may change your mind, young man, after you've heard what I've got to say.'

'What is it, Gran?' asked Ian.

Grandma Elliot clasped her hands, turning and turning the gold wedding band on her finger. 'Where are you going, on your trip?' she asked.

The two men exchanged a look.

'We're taking the kids out to one of the company's oil rigs,' said Mr Madigan.

'Yeah, we're going to sleep on board overnight,' said Frankie, excitedly. 'And when we get to the rig, Ian's going to take *Discovery* in really close –'

'– so that we can take lots of great shots,' added David. 'You see, we all belong to a photography club.'

Grandma Elliot nodded impatiently. 'Yes, yes. And after that? Where are you going after that?' She scowled in Ian's direction. 'It's Devil's Hole, isn't it?'

'I knew it!' growled Ian. 'I knew you'd find out. Sandy's been here, hasn't he?'

'No.' Grandma Elliot laced her fingers together to stop them from trembling. 'Not Sandy.'

'Who then?' Ian leaned forward, his face grim. 'Who's been frightening you?'

7

'I wasn't frightened. Robert would never frighten me.'

Ian stumbled backwards, pressing the back of his hand to his mouth and shaking his head.

'Who's Robert?' whispered Michael, feeling his skin turn cold as he saw how frightened Ian was.

'Robert was my husband, Ian's grandad,' said Grandma Elliot. 'He drowned in Devil's Hole, years ago.'

Frankie and Alice stared at one another with big eyes. David folded his arms more tightly and frowned down at his trainers.

'Mrs Elliot,' said Mr Madigan in a gentle, coaxing voice. 'If your husband drowned years ago, then he couldn't have visited you. That's impossible.'

'Have you never heard of a fetch, Mr Madigan?'

'A . . . fetch?' John Madigan raised his eyebrows at Ian.

'A fetch is the image – the spirit – of a drowned man,' said Ian, stiffly. 'People have seen the fetch of a man appear in his house, dripping wet and silent, at the same time as the man is drowning. Sometimes the fetch reappears at a later date. It's . . .' Ian hesitated. 'It's meant to be a warning. They say if you look in a mirror when the fetch appears, you can see what he's trying to warn you about.'

Frankie looked around at the frightened faces of her friends and swallowed hard. 'What does it do, this fetch?' she asked.

'He goes to someone he loves, usually, or his favourite place. That's right, isn't it, Gran?'

Grandma Elliot rocked on her heels and her milky

eyes stared into the distance. 'I'll never forget that night, the night he drowned,' she said. 'It was late. Everyone else had gone to bed but I couldn't sleep. I was sitting in the parlour by the fire when he came walking in, soaked to the skin and as pale as the moon. "Oh, Robert!" I said. "Did you fall in the harbour?" He would not answer. He did what he always used to do when he came off the boat. He walked up to the fire to warm himself. Then he reached for his pipe and his baccy tin. He reached for them but, of course, he couldn't pick them up. He turned to me then and he gazed into my face and that's when I knew. He looked so sad and lonely, you see. I knew then . . .'

'Poor Robert,' gulped Alice.

'Last night, he came back.'

Ian moved up close to Grandma Elliot, cupping her hands in his. 'Gran, there might be another explanation. It could have been someone else in the house last night, someone who shouldn't have been here. Have you noticed whether anything's gone missing?'

'It was him,' said Grandma Elliot.

'How do you know?'

'He was silent.'

'A burglar would be silent, Gran.'

'All right! I know it was him because . . . because I saw him.' Grandma Elliot turned her blind eyes to Ian and they were full of tears. 'I could see him. I was sitting in the parlour, in the same chair, and I saw him walk in, the same as he always did. Up to the fire he went, reached for the pipe and baccy, then turned to me . . .'

9

'Were you thinking of him?' said Mr Madigan, carefully.

'I think of him every day,' said Grandma Elliot.

'I've heard of that,' said David. 'If you want to see someone enough, your mind can play tricks on you –'

He stopped as Grandma Elliot turned abruptly. 'So. My word is not enough. Please, stand by the front door. All of you.'

'Are you throwing us out?' asked Frankie.

'No, I'm clearing a path.' Grandma Elliot moved confidently over to the door at the back of the room. 'Now. I want you to follow me.' She opened the door and walked through.

Michael was at the front of the group. It was up to him to lead the way after Grandma Elliot but, as he stared through into the darkness beyond the door, he felt a strange reluctance to move out of the sunny kitchen.

'Come on,' hissed David, stepping on his heels.

Michael moved through the doorway into a dark little hall. Straight ahead of him was the back door. The stairs were on his right and, to the left, there was another open door.

'In here,' called Grandma Elliot, from the room beyond the doorway.

Again, Michael hesitated.

'Move!' hissed David behind him.

'Hang on, I can't see yet.'

Yes, that's it, he told himself. That's why I'm waiting. Grandma Elliot did not need sight to move around her cottage. She had gone straight from

10

bright sunshine to semi-darkness without faltering. He needed to adjust.

But even when his eyes had adjusted to the gloom, Michael did not move. It was cold in the hallway, a damp, dreary cold which made his skin come out in goosebumps. And there was that smell . . .

'Michael!'

'OK!'

As Michael stepped into the back room the cold got worse and the smell grew stronger. It was a bad smell. A smell of rotting seaweed, of dead crabs, of stagnant water all mixed up together. It was how he imagined the bottom of the sea would smell, if it were dragged up to the surface.

'Where is it coming from?' whispered David, peering around the little sitting room.

Michael took another step into the room and the carpet squelched under his trainer like a wet sponge.

'The carpet's soaking!' cried Alice, stepping in another wet patch.

'What's going on here, Gran?' asked Ian. 'Has there been a burst pipe or something?'

'No,' said Grandma Elliot calmly from her chair by the fireplace. 'Robert left tracks.'

'What!' Ian flicked on the main light. He crouched, pressed his finger into one of the wet patches, then brought it up to his mouth and touched it with the tip of his tongue. 'Salt,' he said, staring up at Grandma Elliot. He turned to look at Mr Madigan, his face gaunt in the electric light. 'It's sea water.'

'Oh no,' breathed Alice, gazing down at her feet.

The carpet where she stood was dark and wet. She pressed her foot into the carpet pile and saw liquid oozing up around the toe of her boot. The stench rose too, making her gag.

'They move in a line,' said David, from the doorway. 'They start at the back door, along the hall, then into here.' He pointed across the room, showing the direction the tracks took. Everyone stepped back away from his pointing finger to the edges of the room and, finally, the path of the tracks was clear. Dark, wet splodges moved across the floor, from the doorway to the fireplace and Grandma Elliot's chair. In front of the chair, the tracks stopped and one large, wet patch spread out across the carpet, as though someone had stood there in dripping clothes.

'They're still there,' breathed Frankie, pointing to the pipe and tobacco tin on the mantelpiece.

'I've kept them in their place ever since that night,' said Grandma Elliot. She rose from the chair and reached out to touch the pipe. 'He was here,' she said, into the silence. 'Do you believe me now?'

'Yes,' said Michael, and no one contradicted him.

'He's warning us,' said Grandma Elliot. 'It's a warning about Devil's Hole. You have to tell Trident Oil to leave that place alone. Otherwise, I'm warning you, people will die.'

Frankie danced along beside her father, looking up into his face as he descended the steps from Fisherman's Row.

'We're still going, right? Right, Dad?'

'How about watching the steps instead of me, Frankie? Otherwise you won't be going anywhere except the hospital.'

'But we are still going, right?'

'Frankie . . .'

'OK. I'm watching. I just want you to know we've been looking forward to this trip for weeks. Haven't we, guys?'

'Yes,' said David, gazing longingly at *Discovery* as she rocked gently at her mooring.

'Weeks,' said Alice, nudging a silent Michael.

Mr Madigan sighed with relief as Frankie reached the bottom of the steps safely. 'I know that,' he said.

'I have an idea,' said Frankie. 'How about we go to the rig and miss out Devil's Hole, if you're scared?'

Mr Madigan stopped on the quayside next to *Discovery* and the children gathered round him, waiting to hear the fate of their voyage.

'First of all,' said Mr Madigan, 'don't call it Devil's Hole. It has no name on the charts. It's just a sedimentary basin which might have oil at the bottom of it.'

He paused, shading his eyes to watch as Ian Elliot left his grandmother's cottage and hurried along Fisherman's Row. 'Second of all, there is no way I can take you four out for a jaunt on a company survey vessel without an official reason for the voyage. If we go to the rig, we also do the survey. It's a package deal. Still want to go?'

'Yeah!' yelled Frankie.

'Count me in,' said David.

13

Alice looked at Michael, who was staring at Mr Madigan, his eyes big with worry. 'Mr Madigan?' she said. 'What did you think about Grandma Elliot? About the warning?'

Mr Madigan looked at Ian Elliot making his way down the steps. 'Well . . . I think Mrs Elliot misses her husband an awful lot and that's probably why she saw him.'

'But – the sea water . . .' whispered Michael.

'I'm a scientist,' said Mr Madigan firmly. 'I can't let legends and superstitions frighten me off.'

'Yay!' yelled Frankie. 'So we're going!'

'Hold on,' said Mr Madigan. 'There's one more person I need to ask.'

They all turned to watch Ian Elliot walk up to them.

'I've arranged for Gran to stay with my brother while we dry out the cottage,' said Ian.

'Good. Good . . .' Mr Madigan cleared his throat. 'Ian? Do you want to sit this one out? I'd understand if you did. I can always find another pilot.'

Ian hesitated, glancing between Mr Madigan and Grandma Elliot's cottage. 'You don't need to find another pilot,' he said, finally. 'Let's get this boat out of harbour.'

14

2

A gentle tapping woke David. He opened his eyes and frowned into the darkness. His bed was swaying and the wall at his left ear was humming gently. David put out his hand to touch the wall and a steady vibration ran through his fingers. The tapping sounded again, louder this time, then someone opened a door and flicked on the light. David turned his head, screwing up his eyes against the sudden brightness. Two bare feet were resting on his pillow, centimetres from the end of his nose.

David sat up sharply and cracked his skull against the ceiling.

'Hurts, doesn't it?' said Mr Madigan, poking his head over the edge of the bunk. 'I'm always doing that.' He rested his elbows on the mattress and leaned his chin into his hand. 'We're there.'

David was suddenly fully awake. 'The rig!' he yelled.

'Coming up on it now,' said Mr Madigan.

David grinned and threw his pillow down to the other end of the bunk. 'Wake up, smelly feet! We're there!'

Michael lifted his head and peered sleepily at David for a second before his grey eyes grew sharp and focused. He smiled and jumped down to the floor.

'My feet are not smelly,' he said, pulling on his socks.

'Oh, yeah?' said Alice, sticking her head out through the curtains of the bottom bunk. 'You two should have tried sleeping down here next to your trainers.'

She eased out of the narrow space and unfolded her long legs and arms, stretching until the bones cracked.

'Do they smell?' asked Michael uncertainly, frowning at his trainers.

'Do fish swim in the sea?' retorted Alice, drawing herself up to her full height and glaring down her nose at him.

Michael looked at Alice. His hand crept up to pick at the neck of his sweatshirt. His brown hair was sticking up in clumps and his triangular face, always pale, was almost white. Too late, Alice realised that the teasing had gone too far. After years of listening to his father's lectures on boys and dirt, Michael was obsessive about keeping himself clean. Quickly, she wrapped an arm around his thin shoulders and bent to whisper in his ear.

'Only joking.'

'I knew that,' said Michael, smiling with relief.

'Coming through,' yelled Frankie, rolling out under the bunk curtains and landing on Mr Madigan's foot. She grinned up at him and her eyes shone. 'Hi, Dad.'

'Life jackets,' winced Mr Madigan, tipping Frankie

16

off his foot and hobbling to the door. He pointed to the orange safety gear piled up in the corner of the cabin and scowled fiercely. 'If anyone so much as puts a toe out on deck without one of those on, you can forget your photography project. You'll be confined to quarters for the rest of the voyage.'

All four of them dived for the life jackets. Mr Madigan nodded in satisfaction and left the cabin.

Frankie held one up against her chest. 'Now just how am I going to brighten up this dull old thing?'

'But – it's fluorescent orange,' said Alice.

'Gotcha!' laughed Frankie. 'Come on. Last one on deck's a monkey's bum.'

They grabbed their cameras and raced up the steps from the cabin, clambering over the high metal step of the doorframe and out on to the black rubberised surface of the fore-deck.

It was barely dawn. Sea and sky merged together in smudges of navy and charcoal. They shivered in the cold wind as they hurried up to the fore-deck, David in the lead.

'Wow!' said David, coming to a stop. His mouth dropped open in amazement. He was used to working with large machinery. He could climb up the side of a grain silo as tall as a house, he could drive a combine harvester as big as a brontosaurus, but they were nothing compared to this.

The oil rig towered in front of him, huge and dark against the pale dawn sky. Eight massive steel legs rose above the grey surface of the sea, reinforced by a complex scaffolding which criss-crossed the spaces between them. The square bulk of the platform rested on these eight legs, giving the rig a top-heavy look, like an old woman with her skirts hitched up for a paddle. A long sloping flare stack and a loading crane elbowed out on each side of the rig, and an octagonal helipad, in green and yellow stripes, was perched on top like a Sunday hat.

'It's as big as a town!' yelled Frankie, coming up beside David.

'Look at those colours,' breathed Michael, staring at the brilliant tracery of orange, white and blue lights which frosted the platform. 'They'd make a great photograph.'

'They're OK,' said David. 'But I'm going for the work. I should be able to get some good shots of the drilling platform with this.' Gently, he eased his prized telephoto lens from the case and fitted it to his camera.

Alice hopped on to the deck last, still struggling to force her foot into a trainer with hopelessly knotted laces. She grabbed the rail, gave a final stamp and the trainer was on. Only then did she lift her head to look at the rig. With a gasp, she staggered backwards and sat down on the deck.

Michael hurried over and looked into her face, which was as pale as a mushroom and shiny with sweat. 'The usual?' he asked.

Alice nodded and her head reeled.

'What's up?' said Mr Madigan. 'Surely you can't be sea-sick, not after all this time?'

'No,' said Michael, still looking at Alice. 'It's the rig. She doesn't like high things. What do you want to do? Go below? I'll come with you, if you like.'

Alice gave Michael a grateful smile. 'No. I'll be fine if I don't look at it.'

'But what about your photographs?'

Alice turned her back on the oil rig and stood up. 'There's plenty going on right here,' she said, sweeping her arm around the deck.

They each settled to work on their chosen ideas as the survey vessel circled the rig. Alice could hear the pounding thud of heavy machinery and the shouts of the oil men, but she did not turn around. Instead, she took shot after shot of David, Frankie and Michael in their orange life jackets, of Mr Madigan patrolling the deck, and of Ian Elliot peering out through the windows of the control room as he piloted *Discovery*.

When the sun rose twenty minutes later, it brought with it a strengthening wind. Ian Elliot looked at the way the waves were beginning to crash against the support legs of the rig and decided it was time to move off.

'That's your lot!' called Mr Madigan as *Discovery* turned. 'Now, who's for some breakfast?'

They hurried below to the warmth of the galley. Mr Madigan handed out bowls of creamy porridge while, out on the deserted deck, the cold song of the wind grew stronger and spray began to break over the rails. Behind *Discovery*, the huge square bulk of the oil rig faded into the distance until even the torch of burning gas at the end of the flare stack shrank to a pinpoint of light and blinked out. *Discovery* rode the swells alone, a single orange dot suspended between the pale grey sky and the steely grey water.

*   *   *

19

'I'm glad we're in here,' said Michael, peering through the spray-spattered glass of the control-room windows. Outside, the wind whined and howled around the radio mast and freezing sea water washed over the decks.

'Me too,' muttered Ian Elliot, glancing up from his instrument panel. *Discovery* see-sawed over a swell and Michael staggered, causing Ian to give him a critical look. 'Son, promise me you'll move away from all this fancy navigational equipment if your porridge starts coming up again.'

'I won't be sick,' promised Michael. 'I like it out here.'

'Do you now? Some people find it boring.'

'How can they find the sea boring?' asked Michael.

Ian gave him a surprised look, then his face relaxed into a smile. 'I can't understand it either,' he said.

They stood together in silence, both looking out at the horizon. Ian moved his hand to the tiller and rested it there, even though *Discovery* was on auto-pilot.

'I bet you'd be good at fishing,' said Ian after a while.

'I've never tried it. But I'd like to,' said Michael.

'Good.' Ian winked at him, then turned back to his instrument panel.

'What do all these dials and things do?' asked Michael.

'They drive this thing without me,' laughed Ian. 'Once I've told them which way to go.'

'But what if it all goes wrong?'

'Don't worry, I've still got the tiller here. The auto-pilot's pretty good on longer voyages, though, once I've set the course. Over there, that's the Satnav computer.'

'Satellite navigation?' guessed Michael.

'You've got it. But I still have my charts too. See, on the table.'

Michael looked at the charts. A smooth round stone was resting on top of them, holding them down. He reached over and picked it up.

'That is heavy!' he said, surprised at the weight in his hand.

'It's heavy because it's got a high metal content,' said Ian. 'Do you know what it is?'

'No.'

'That's a ballast stone. I found it in the old harbour. They used those in the early sailing ships. They stowed them down in the hold if they had a small cargo, to keep the ship in balance. Then, when they reached a harbour where they were picking up more cargo, they would dump some of the ballast stones on the pile, ready for the next ship to use.'

Michael carefully put the ballast stone back on top of the charts. 'I wonder if it feels out of place, in amongst all this fancy equipment?'

Ian laughed. 'Want to know what the rest of this stuff does?'

Michael nodded and moved to stand next to him.

'Right. Those are the electronic log and the radar and sonar screens over there. The sonar builds up a picture of the sea bed and the radar does the same job above the water. It tells me what else is sailing around out here, apart from us.'

Fascinated, Michael watched the radar screen as the line swept around the circle again and again. Green patterns played across his face in the dimly lit room.

'See that green blob there?' asked Ian, pointing to the edge of the radar screen. 'That's a big container ship, heading for Norway.'

'There you go,' said Mr Madigan, behind them. Michael turned to see Frankie, Alice and David clustered around another monitor. Michael edged in beside Alice, who moved over to let him see the brightly coloured pattern on the monitor screen.

'What is it?' asked David.

'That's the official reason for this voyage,' said Mr Madigan. 'It's a photograph taken from a satellite, hundreds of kilometres up in space.'

'Amazing,' breathed David, leaning forward to stare at the circle of dark water, set against a pale blue background.

'That is what we geoscientists call a sedimentary basin,' said Mr Madigan. 'It's like a hole in the sea bed. This particular one looks very deep – see how dark the water is on the satellite photograph? Nobody knows quite how far down it goes. That's what we're going to survey.'

'Do you think there's any oil at the bottom?' asked Alice.

'There should be, but the oil company needs me to check it out before they start all that expensive drilling.'

'You should tell them not to bother,' muttered Ian Elliot.

'Not that again,' sighed Mr Madigan. 'You agreed to pilot this trip –'

Ian shrugged. 'So now I can't say what I think?'

'OK. Give me some facts.'

'Facts? What can I say? It has a strangeness about it. Sometimes, you can take a boat in there and the water's teeming with fish. Packed with them! Other times, not a single one.'

'Come on, Ian,' sighed Mr Madigan. 'Shoals of fish move around. That's not strange.'

'Maybe not. But Devil's Hole is strange.'

'Don't tease them, Ian,' said Mr Madigan, glancing at Michael's wide grey eyes.

'Who's teasing? It has its own weather, for a start. Devil's Hole can be calm when the sea around it is like a pot on the boil. Or a sea fret'll form there – just there, mind – on a bright day. Strange currents, too. Very strange.' Ian hesitated, glancing at the children and then back to Mr Madigan. 'And you already know boats have been lost in Devil's Hole with no explanation.'

Mr Madigan folded his arms. 'Ian, why did you come on this trip, if you feel so bad about the place?'

'Because I know it! I couldn't let you come out here without me! Talk about lambs to the slaughter –'

'Ian! I think we've heard enough.' Mr Madigan ruffled Alice's hair and gave Frankie a quick hug. 'All we're doing today is checking it out. OK, guys? How far, Ian?'

Ian turned his back on Mr Madigan. 'We're coming up on it now,' he said gruffly.

'Right. You four can watch, but don't get in the way. We've got to get a seismic survey going here and –'

Mr Madigan stopped as *Discovery* gave a sudden lurch. The engines roared beneath them and Ian leapt for the instrument panel, moving with a speed which was surprising in such a big man.

'Are we safe?' whispered Michael, twisting at the ties of his life jacket.

'We're fine,' said Ian, bringing the roar of the engines back down to a rumble. 'The wind dropped and the sea calmed, all of a sudden. *Discovery* had too much engine power with nothing to push against, so she shot off like a cork from a bottle. Caught us by surprise, that's all. It was just as we sailed into Devil's Hole,' he added, glancing at John Madigan over the heads of the children.

Told you, his glance said.

'All right,' said Mr Madigan brightly. 'Panic over. Keep heading for the centre. We'll start the survey there.'

'Um . . . I think . . .' David's voice was so faint that they all turned to look at him. He was standing with his back to the windows and his face was blank with shock.

'What do you think?' asked Frankie.

'I think there's something . . .' David faltered a second time and looked at them uncertainly. Alice felt her spine prickle. David was never unsure about anything. She glanced over at Michael. He, too, knew

24

something was wrong. He was watching David with a mixture of astonishment and horror as though the solid ground beneath his feet had suddenly cracked apart.

'Yeah?' prompted Frankie, still unaware of the growing tension.

David turned stiffly, forcing himself to take a second look at the deck through the control room windows. 'Yes,' he said. 'There is. There's something out there.'

A silence fell as the others in the room turned to the windows. Outside, a sea mist had crept up on *Discovery*, rising stealthily from the surface of the water and wrapping the vessel in a grey shroud. But that was not what David was talking about. He pointed at the deck rails, which were coiled around with sickly green, luminous tentacles. The radio mast was wreathed in them. Sheets of the pale green stuff shifted and shimmered on the deck.

'Dad . . . ?' said Frankie, glancing fearfully at the green tentacles. 'Is it – alive?'

'No. And there's nothing strange about it, either,' said Mr Madigan. 'It's natural. A naturally occurring phosphorescence you sometimes get at sea.'

'Phospho– what?' said David.

'A sort of light. It's electrostatic, I think. Something to do with the weather conditions.'

'Saint Elmo's fire,' breathed Ian, wiping the sweat from his forehead. 'That's what it's called. It foretells a death.'

'That's only an old fishing superstition,' snapped

25

Mr Madigan. 'Now, Ian, I'd appreciate it if you'd give up on frightening –'

Mr Madigan stopped speaking as all the monitor screens in the control room went black. Suddenly, the only light came from the pale green curtains slithering across the outside of the windows. Alice yelped as the short-wave radio beside her gave off a high-pitched shriek.

'What's happening, Dad?' shouted Frankie, grabbing at Mr Madigan's arm.

John Madigan glanced from the shimmering green deck to the row of blank screens to the shrieking radio. 'Honey, I don't know,' he said, shaking his head. 'I just don't know.'

Ian Elliot turned a dial on the radio and the shrieking stopped. 'We need to get out of here,' he muttered, his fingers jumping from dial to dial in an attempt to bring his instrument panel back to life.

'Don't worry. There's an explanation for this,' said Mr Madigan, moving along the row of computer monitors with Frankie still clinging to his arm. He checked all the connections and tapped at a keyboard. 'There's always an explanation . . .'

'Please, can we go?' whispered Alice, glancing at the green-lit windows.

'I daren't move with the equipment down,' said Ian. 'I've lost everything and we're blind in this sea fret. Give me a minute to check the charts first.' He turned to the chart table and stopped, staring down at the compass.

'Will you look at that?' he said. He picked up the compass and held it out towards them. They could all see the red-tipped pointer spinning back and forth around the dial.

'There must be an explanation –' began Mr Madigan.

'You keep saying that, man, but I don't hear you coming up with one!' Ian shook his head and turned back to his charts.

David walked over to stand beside Alice. Michael edged closer to Ian Elliot. He wanted to grab hold of the big man's arm the way Frankie was hanging on to her father, but he contented himself with pretending to study the radar screen. As he watched, the blank screen suddenly lit up, at the same time as the monitor screens behind him blinked into life.

'Hey!' cried Mr Madigan, lifting his hands away from his keyboard. 'I think I'm getting somewhere. What about you, Ian?'

Ian Elliot looked over at the radar screen, just as the flickering image went dark.

'Aw!' sighed Mr Madigan. 'They've all crashed again.'

'Did you see anything, son?' Ian asked Michael, nodding at the radar screen.

'Oh, yes. It did come on. The radar did a couple of sweeps before it blacked out again. The image wasn't very clear, but there was this fuzzy green blob –'

Suddenly, Ian was beside Michael, gripping his shoulder. 'A blob?'

'Yes.'

Ian's big hand gripped harder. 'Are you sure it wasn't that container ship I showed you earlier?'

'No. It was in a different place.'

'Where, exactly?'

Michael pressed a finger to the spot on the screen where he had seen the blob.

'That's slap in the middle of Devil's Hole,' muttered Ian. 'You're right, son. It's not the container ship.'

'It was about the same size, though,' said Michael.

'The same – !' Ian Elliot slammed his palm down on a red button and they all jumped as a howling wail rang out just above their heads. Ian lifted his hand from the button and the howl moaned away into silence.

'What's happening?' asked David.

'Shhh!' hissed Mr Madigan, moving to stand beside Ian Elliot. Both men listened and strained their eyes to peer through the grey mist outside.

'No answering foghorn,' said Mr Madigan, 'so it can't be a ship. What else could show up that big?'

Ian sounded the foghorn again, then turned his attention back to Michael. 'You say it was moving towards us?'

'I – I don't know.' Michael was scared now and his voice came out thin and high. 'It was moving towards the middle of the circle –'

'That's us. How could you tell it was moving?'

'It was quite a bit nearer the middle on the second sweep.'

'Sounds like it's travelling fast, whatever it is,' said Mr Madigan.

'Get us out of here!' wailed Frankie.

'Right.' Ian stepped up to the control panel and took hold of the tiller. The engine note rose and *Discovery* began to turn in a tight circle.

'What are you doing?' asked Mr Madigan.

'I'm going to turn us around and head back the way we came in. I don't need charts or a compass to do that.'

David raced to the window at the back of the control room which gave him a view of the stern of the boat. The other three followed and they all watched the grey wall of mist beyond the stern. They stood close together, frightened and quiet. Something as big as a ship was out there and it was heading straight for them.

'Hurry!' cried Frankie, as *Discovery* finished her turn. The survey boat wallowed for a few seconds, her propellers churning.

'We're not moving!' shouted Alice, staring out at the lazily swirling mist.

'Inertia,' said Ian, shortly.

'What?'

'He means it always takes a while to get a boat this size going,' said David. He managed to keep his voice calm but his leg muscles were jumping with the useless urge to run.

Slowly, sluggishly, *Discovery* began to make headway. Michael willed the boat to go faster, gripping the rim of the window so hard, his fingertips turned white. Finally, *Discovery* picked up speed and surged forward, cutting through the mist.

'Hurry!' begged Alice, near to tears.

'Yes, hurry!' echoed David, and suddenly they were all shouting as the panic took hold.

'Come on. Come on!'

'It must be right behind us!'

'Come on –'

Frankie stopped in mid-shout and they all staggered as the boat lurched.

'It's got us,' whispered Michael, covering his face. He waited for the hull to splinter, for icy sea water to pour into the room. Nothing happened.

It was Alice who gently pulled his hands away from his eyes and steered him to the window.

'Look,' she said.

Michael looked and saw the sky. *Discovery* had broken free of the mist and was back out on the open sea. The widening strip of water between the boat and the sea-fret was empty, apart from a churning white line of wake. Nothing was following them as they pulled away from Devil's Hole. Wordlessly, they shared a look of relief. The wind found the radio mast and started up a song, breaking the silence.

'We're up and running again,' said Mr Madigan as the computer monitors blinked on. Ian concentrated on his radar screen, re-adjusting the dials until the green and black image was sharp and clear. They gathered round, watching the line sweep an empty circle while Ian quietly checked out the sonar screen too.

'I did see a blob,' whispered Michael.

'I'm sure you did, son,' said Ian. 'But it's gone now, whatever it was.'

3

The clouds cleared on the homeward voyage and *Discovery* chugged into harbour in the middle of a mild spring afternoon. Sunlight surfed the wavetops and the whole sky was pearly blue. It was hard to believe that they had been sailing through a grey world of wind and spray just a few hours earlier.

Even when *Discovery* was tied up to the quayside, rocking gently to the rhythm of the waves, the children stayed on board. Ian and Mr Madigan were locked in the control room, trying to figure out what had happened to the equipment in Devil's Hole, so the four of them sat together on the fore-deck, catching the late afternoon sun as they waited for David's mum to arrive. Frankie leaned over the rail, looking down on the holiday-makers as they strolled along the quayside.

'They have no idea, do they?' she sighed.

'No idea of what?' asked David.

'Of what it's like out there.'

David laughed. 'One boat trip, and she thinks she's Christopher Columbus.'

Frankie looked hurt for a few seconds, then her mouth turned up at the corners and spoiled the effect. 'But what a voyage, Davey! And, hey, I think we got through it pretty well.'

'Got through what?' asked Michael quietly. 'What exactly *did* we get through out there? No one's talking about what happened.'

Alice gave Michael a worried glance. He was sitting hunched up in the shade with his back against the control room wall.

'Don't worry about it,' she said, sitting down next to him. 'We're home now.'

A muscle was jumping just below his eye. Michael pressed his fingers to it and took a shaky breath. 'But what happened?'

David frowned and folded his arms. 'Nothing happened, except we all got into a stupid panic over a bit of fog. We let the stories get to us. That's all.'

Michael did not answer so David stepped in front of him, blocking his view of the sea. Michael stared right through him, his grey eyes dark and unfocused. Alice looked at his eyes and shivered as a sea breeze lifted the hairs on the back of her neck.

David kicked Michael's foot, hard. 'I said, it was only a bit of fog!'

Michael drew his knees up to his chest, moving his feet out of harm's way. 'A bit of fog? All right, David. How do you explain that bit of fog?'

'What do you want, a weather forecast?'

'The fog was only at Devil's Hole. Nowhere else.'

Alice looked at David, trying to understand why he was so angry. 'Calm down, you two,' she pleaded, but they both ignored her.

'OK. All right. I can explain the mist,' said David. 'If you get deeper – much deeper – water all of a sudden, like at Devil's Hole, then it'll be colder than the surrounding sea, right? So you get low-lying mist above the colder water.'

Frankie shrugged. 'That makes sense,' she said.

David leaned on the rail and smiled smugly. 'See? There's always an explanation for everything.'

'Then why hasn't Mr Elliot got an explanation for Devil's Hole?' asked Michael. 'He knows these waters much better than Frankie's dad. He's been sailing in them since he was a little boy. He can't explain it, but he knows Devil's Hole is a bad place. I think we should have listened to him and left it alone.'

Frankie bristled like a hedgehog. 'Hey! Are you saying my dad was in the wrong today, you little creep!'

'People do get things wrong,' said Michael, quietly. 'Even fathers.'

'Yeah?'

'Come on, you three,' said Alice. 'We shouldn't be arguing like this. Let's try and be a bit more grown up –'

Alice stopped as the control room door slammed open. Mr Madigan stormed out on to the deck, with Ian Elliot close behind.

'I can't believe it!' shouted Ian. 'You put these children in danger today because you wouldn't listen to me. And now you're planning to go out there again, after what happened?'

'They were not in danger. And of course we'll

33

be going back out there,' yelled Mr Madigan. 'It's our job!'

The two men glared at one another across the deck.

'What is it about you and that patch of water?' shouted Mr Madigan.

Ian Elliot looked at his friend, then lowered himself to the deck beside Michael. He spread his big, scarred hands over his knees. 'My grandfather had hands like this,' he said. 'Fisherman's hands.'

Ian said nothing more for a long time. He stared down at his hands and the others stared too. They studied the reddened skin of his knuckles and the scattering of coppery hairs and they waited for him to speak. At last, Ian took a deep breath and looked up at Mr Madigan.

'Devil's Hole took my grandfather. It killed my grandfather. I'm scared of the place. That's the simple truth.'

Frankie sat down on the other side of Ian and put her hand over his.

David cleared his throat. 'Mr Elliot – I don't want to be rude but, I mean, fishermen do drown sometimes. It could've happened anywhere, couldn't it?'

Ian shook his head. 'Not the way my grandad died.'

'How did he die?'

'David!' hissed Alice, glaring at him.

'It's all right,' smiled Ian. 'I'll tell you about it. It may make you think twice about going out there again, John.'

'I'll listen,' said Mr Madigan, finding a seat on the deck. 'That's all I'm promising.'

David was the only one left standing. He moved a little way off from the others and sat turned slightly away from them.

'I was mad with my grandad the evening he went out to Devil's Hole,' admitted Ian. 'I wanted to go with him but he said I was too young for the night fishing. I was still mad with him when he left that evening to catch the tide, so I wouldn't say goodbye. Ten minutes later, I was regretting it. I jumped on my bike and raced down to the end of the harbour wall to catch his boat as she sailed through. I could see him in the wheelhouse. I waved to him and he lifted his cap and whirled it around his head. I think he knew I was sorry. I hope he did.'

Ian sighed, tugging at his beard as he remembered. 'I was eleven years old and he was forty-eight. He seemed very old to me then. But now I'm nearly the same age as he was, and I know he wasn't old at all.

'They fished all night without much luck and, in the early hours of the morning, Grandad decided to try Devil's Hole.'

'Why did he do that, when he must have heard the stories about boats disappearing?' asked Michael.

'Oh, yes, he knew about the disappearances,' said Ian. 'But empty nets meant no money for him or the crew, and there were also the other stories about record catches in Devil's Hole. So he took a chance. That's all. The fishing is always about taking chances, one way or another.

'Another fisherman picked up a Mayday message on his radio. It was very faint and breaking up, but he recognised my grandfather's voice. He swears my grandfather was yelling something about – well, about the sea boiling . . .'

'Boiling?' said David. 'Did he mean boiling hot?'

'No, I don't think so. I think he meant the surface was heaving and bubbling as if something –' Ian stopped abruptly and waved his hand in front of his mouth, as though to brush away the words he had come so close to saying. He glanced at Michael out of the corner of his eye, then continued the story.

'By the time the lifeboat got there, the sea was calm and there was no sign of my grandfather's boat. They never found any wreckage. Or bodies.'

'What happened to them?' asked Frankie.

'I don't know,' said Ian.

'You must have a theory,' said David.

Ian shook his head. 'No. I leave that to other folk. There's plenty willing to give you theories by the bucketful.'

Mr Madigan got to his feet with a sigh. 'I'm sorry about your grandad, Ian, but I have to do this survey. My offer's still open, though. If you want to duck out of this one, I'll understand. I can get another pilot assigned to the project.'

'Duck out?' Ian folded his arms and gave his friend a hurt look. 'Another pilot?'

'Look, I only meant –'

'I won't duck out. I'll pilot *Discovery* for you, John, if you're determined to go out again. You'll stand a better chance with a local man out there. Besides, this survey might tell me what I've always wanted to know – how my grandfather died.'

A car horn from the quayside broke the silence.

36

'That'll be Mum,' said David. 'She always does that triple hoot.'

Michael, Alice and David went below to collect their bags. Mr Madigan was already working at one of the monitors when they returned to the control room and his only response to their thanks and goodbyes was an absent-minded wave.

'Boy, am I in for a fun night,' sighed Frankie as Ian helped them all off the boat. 'He's still trying to work out why all the equipment crashed. He'll be like that now until he's solved the problem.'

'He sounds just like someone else I know,' said David, waving to his mum over in the quayside car park.

'What do you mean?'

'Frankie, you know what I mean. You're just like him.'

'Yeah, yeah,' sighed Frankie. She was looking unusually sombre as Ian set her down on the quayside. David watched her and wished he could take back his words. He took a step towards Frankie and walked into something. A bolt of horrified embarrassment shot through him as he realised he was standing with his face squashed up against Ian Elliot's chest. Quickly, he tried to right himself and staggered backwards, sitting down hard on the quayside.

Puzzled, Alice leaned down to give David a hand and found herself tipping forward over his outstretched legs.

'Ouch!' said David as Alice fell across his knees.

'What's wrong with them?' asked Frankie.

'You've got it too, I'm afraid,' said Ian.

'What?'

'Walk over to that lobster pot – in a straight line,' ordered Ian.

'That's easy,' said Frankie. She set off confidently, but the smooth concrete of the quayside kept playing tricks on her feet, slamming up against the soles of her boots, or dropping away altogether.

Behind her, Ian started snorting with laughter.

'What's happening?' asked Frankie, bracing her knees to steady herself.

'Give it a few minutes,' laughed Ian. 'You've been at sea for twenty-four hours. Your brains think you're still out there. You need to get your land legs back, that's all.'

David, Alice and Frankie immediately began to wobble around the quayside and soon they were so weak with laughter they could hardly stand up. Michael ignored the fun. He stood by the bags, quiet and withdrawn.

'All right, son?' asked Ian.

'I did see something,' said Michael, scuffing the concrete with the toe of his trainer. 'On the radar screen.'

Ian bent close to his ear and whispered, 'I know you did.'

Michael smiled quickly, then stopped as his chin started to quiver. 'But I wish I hadn't. I wish I'd seen nothing at all.' He turned away from Ian and wiped the sleeve of his jacket across his face.

'Tell you what,' said Ian, standing next to Michael without looking at him. 'You're on your Easter holidays. I've got time on my hands tomorrow while

38

Frankie's dad checks out the boat. Why don't you meet me here in the morning and we'll do some fishing over at the old harbour?'

Michael smiled up at Ian. 'Yes, please.'

'Yaaay, fishing!' yelled Frankie.

'Only quiet folk allowed,' growled Ian, rolling his eyes at Michael.

'I can be quiet,' said Frankie in an exaggerated whisper. 'What time?'

'Very, very early,' said Ian, but Frankie only grinned.

David and Alice looked at one another. Alice flapped her hands at David, urging him forward. David shrugged and did as he was told. 'Um, Mr Elliot?' he began. 'Can we –?'

'All right, all right,' sighed Ian, waving at David's mother as she got out of her car. 'I'll meet you all in the old harbour tomorrow, early. Now go on, you're keeping your mum waiting.'

Ian kept up his scowl as Michael, Alice and David were driven off in the car and Frankie clambered back on board *Discovery*. Only when they were all gone did he let his face smooth out into a look of sadness.

He walked along the quayside to the spot where the fishing boats were moored. Their high, snub-nosed bows nudged one another and nodded together in a secretive huddle. Their wheelhouses stood like sentry boxes. Ian climbed down the rusty quayside ladder and on to one of the boats. He stood in the stern and breathed in the spinachy smell of seaweed and listened to the slip-slop of the waves.

His grandfather had gone out on a night just like

this. He had piloted his boat past the little red-and-white striped lighthouse at the harbour mouth and he had never come back. Ian Elliot gazed out at the dark sea, swept by the clear white beam of the lighthouse lamp, and he wondered whether the same fate waited for him.

David had the road to himself as he cycled to the harbour early the next morning. He stopped at the top of the hill which led down into town and sat for a few minutes, enjoying the view. Behind him, the family farm spread out along the river bank, each field tucked under a blanket of early-morning mist. Ahead of him, the town slept at the base of the hill, secure within the high walls which ringed it. David let his gaze follow the curve of the river as it flowed under the Royal Border Bridge, skirted the town and emptied itself into the harbour. If he screwed up his eyes, he could just see the orange dot which was *Discovery*.

David frowned. He had learned something from his time out at sea. He preferred the land. Land was something he knew about and that made him feel secure. David shook his head in embarrassment over his reactions in Devil's Hole the previous day. He was sure he would never have panicked over a stupid patch of fog if his feet had been on solid ground instead of on the deck of a boat.

David pushed off and began to coast down the long hill, casting smug glances at all the closed curtains in the houses he passed. There was no way Alice, Michael and Frankie would be up this early.

He imagined how it would be when he reached the harbour. He would cycle on to the quayside and swing easily out of the saddle as he reached the lonely figure of Ian Elliot. 'Farmers and fishermen, Ian,' he would say. 'We're the only ones who know how to get up in the morning.'

The reality was even better than David had imagined. Further along the harbour, a small group of local fishermen were getting ready to put out, but the quayside in front of *Discovery* was completely empty. He had reached the harbour before any of them, even Ian. Quietly, David chained his bike to a bench on the quayside in front of *Discovery*, then he sat on the bench and tried to look as though he had been waiting for hours.

Further down the quayside, the cluster of fishermen began to move towards their boats, waving and shouting to one another. David gave them a casual glance and froze, staring at the two figures – one big, one small – who had broken away from the rest of the group and were now strolling along the quayside towards him, carrying a bucket between them.

'Michael!' gasped David, getting to his feet. 'But . . .'

Michael was extremely good at reading faces and his welcoming smile began to falter as he got closer to David. Quickly, David dumped his expression of annoyed surprise and replaced it with one of mild interest.

'What's in there?' he asked, pointing to the bucket.

'Bait,' said Ian, showing David a slimy pink and silver mess made up of fish heads and other unidentifiable chunks. 'Odds and ends from the boats. I was going to dig for lug worms, but this one didn't fancy using live bait. Did you, son?'

Michael shook his head, still watching David anxiously. His face was pale and there were dark smudges under his eyes.

It looks like he hardly slept, thought David. No wonder he was down here earlier than me. A feeling of shame crept over David. He swallowed his hurt pride and put his arm around Michael's shoulders. 'Come on, then,' he said. 'Let's get some fishing in before Frankie arrives and scares them all off.'

'Too late, buddy,' yawned Frankie from the deck of *Discovery*.

Ian smiled up at her. 'Trouble! I'm impressed. I didn't think you'd get up this early.'

'Yeah, well . . .' Frankie slumped against the rail and closed her eyes. 'Just don't ask me to do it again.'

'And here's the fourth,' said Ian as Alice loped along the quayside towards them, her long black hair swinging back and forth in rhythm with her steps. David and Michael turned together, and smiled, and waved. Frankie grinned.

'OK, guys, break it up. Let's go fish.'

'First we need to get the rods,' said Ian. 'I've got a couple stored up at Gran's cottage. We can check the place out while we're there.'

Michael stopped smiling. 'Check it out?'

'That's right,' said Ian, leading the way to the steps. 'We've had the back windows open and the storage heaters going for two nights now. It should be just about dried out in there. I hope so. Gran's giving us a hard time. She's itching to move back in.'

Michael lagged behind all the way up the steps and along the lane to the cottage. Alice fell back to join him as Ian produced a key and unlocked the front door.

'You could sit out here and wait for us,' she said, softly.

Michael had been thinking of doing just that, but now he straightened his shoulders and quickened his step.

'Of course I'll go in,' he said.

The smell hit them as soon as Ian pushed open the door. It was the same cold, dead smell – the smell of something dragged to the surface from the bottom of the sea – but it was much worse.

Ian scowled, pressing the back of his hand to his nose. 'This isn't right . . .'

They were all covering their noses, trying not to breathe in, but the smell still got through, coating the back of their throats and making them choke.

'I don't understand it,' coughed Ian. 'It should've dried up by now.'

'Maybe we ought to leave,' whispered Michael.

David glared at him. 'Don't be stupid. What are you frightened of? It's a damp house! That's all! And it needs sorting before it gets any worse.'

David marched across Grandma Elliot's kitchen and was through the door to the back of the house before anyone could stop him. He stumbled, sun-blinded, into the sitting room. The carped squelched under his feet and the stench rose in suffocating waves. David clamped a hand over his face. The storage heater behind him was throwing out a strong heat, he could feel it on the back of his legs, but the room was as cold as a cave. As he stood still, waiting for his eyes to adjust to the dimness, David felt a deep sadness steal over him. It seeped up through the soles of his feet and wrapped itself around his heart. He clutched a hand to his chest and took a shaky breath.

'I'm so sorry,' he said.

There was a click behind him and brightness pounced into the room.

'What did you say?' asked Frankie.

'Nothing,' muttered David, shading his eyes against the light and turning away.

'This is gross!' said Frankie, picking her way across the carpet to the fireplace.

'It's worse,' said Alice from the doorway.

'The back-yard drain must be blocked,' said Ian. 'I'll go and check.'

Michael edged into the room with a look of relief on his face. 'The drains! Of course. That would explain the smell and the wet floor.'

'Yeah, but it doesn't explain this,' said Frankie, pointing to the mantelpiece.

They all crowded together to look. Robert's pipe and tobacco tin were sitting in a pool of water. The rest of the mantelpiece was dry.

David stared at the tobacco tin. A sob began to swell at the back of his throat. He swallowed hard, turned and stumbled from the room.

They found him sitting on the low wall outside the

cottage when they came out with the fishing rods a few minutes later. The sun was warming the wall but David was shivering.

'Are you OK?' asked Alice, sitting next to him.

David shrugged. 'Cold seems to have got into my bones.'

'You'll live,' said Frankie callously, hauling him to his feet. 'Now, get your sweet self down to the old harbour. Ian says it's too early to start calling plumbers and stuff, so he's going to set us up with a bit of sea fishing!'

'I don't know,' mumbled David. 'I'm not sure I feel like fishing . . .'

'Well I think it's just what we need,' said Alice, linking arms with David and Michael. 'An ordinary day.'

4

Alice was right. An ordinary day was just what they needed. And they very nearly got one. Ian taught them how to bait their hooks and cast safely, then he left them to it. No one mentioned Devil's Hole or Grandma Elliot's cottage all day. Michael became completely absorbed in the battle to catch a fish. Alice and David divided their time between fishing, rock-pooling, searching for fossils in the Borderland rocks and paddling in the icy water. Frankie flitted back and forth over the harbour wall, never settling for long but always returning to the old harbour, once bringing packages of hot salty chips and cold drinks.

The sun was low in the sky when Ian reappeared, climbing over the harbour wall and down the rocks into the bay with Frankie beside him.

'So, have you caught anything?' asked Frankie.

'Nothing yet,' muttered David.

'I caught a flappie,' said Michael proudly.

'A what?'

'A flappie is what people round here call a flatfish,' said David in his explaining voice. 'It's a flounder, actually.'

'It's in there,' said Michael, nodding his head towards a bucket filled with sea water.

Frankie inspected the catch, clearly unimpressed. 'Back home, my dad went out for tuna. When they got back to harbour, they strung up the one my dad caught and it was as tall as me.'

'Not very big, then?' said David, looking down his nose at the top of Frankie's head.

'Oh, ha ha ha. My go,' said Frankie, holding her hand out for the fishing rod. David sighed and pretended to be reluctant but, secretly, he was pleased to take a break. He eased his shoulders and climbed up the rocks to sit beside Alice on the harbour wall.

'Watch this, Frankie,' said Michael eagerly. 'Now, see how I'm keeping the bait as close to those rocks as I can without getting tangled up in them?'

'You are? Why?'

Michael's eyes shone with excitement. 'Mr Elliot says there might be cod by those rocks. They come in here to feed when there aren't any seals about. Wouldn't it be great to catch one?'

'Great,' echoed Frankie unconvincingly.

'Had enough?' asked Ian, looking up at David.

'Yes,' admitted David. 'Sorry.'

'No, that's fine,' said Ian. 'You either take to the fishing or you don't. Now him,' he added, nodding towards Michael, 'he's a natural.'

'How do you mean?'

'You think fishing is a lot of standing about doing nothing,' said Ian, squinting up at David. 'That's why you're bored. But Michael there, his mind's working all the time, thinking about those fish out by the rocks. He's guessing how the sunlight on the surface of the water looks to them. He's figuring out how to

47

move the bait to make it seem like food rather than a threat. He's getting a feel for the currents and the best places to cast. Do you see what I mean?'

David shrugged. 'I suppose so,' he said in a bewildered voice.

Ian laughed and stowed the cardboard box he had brought with him in the shade. 'Like I said, you either take to it or you don't.' He moved down the beach to join Michael and Frankie.

'Look at Michael!' said Alice. 'He's so happy and – well, dirty . . .'

David looked and saw what Alice meant. The sleeves of Michael's sweatshirt were shoved up past his elbows and the front was smeared with fish blood and slime where he had wiped his hands after baiting his hook. The legs of his jeans were soaked to the knee and his hair was sticking up all over the place. He looked like any other boy.

'I'm glad he's OK,' said Alice. 'I thought he'd still be upset . . . about what happened yesterday.'

'Nothing happened yesterday,' said David gruffly. 'We got a bit scared and a bit silly, that's all.'

'Yes,' said Alice carefully. 'I've been thinking the same thing.'

Just then Michael gave an excited shout as his rod curved into a bow. He had finally caught his cod. It broke surface, leaping, jumping and twisting in rainbow arcs of spray as he slowly reeled it into shore. The others gathered around him, yelling with excitement and shouting encouragement, but Michael was totally absorbed in bringing in his fish.

Ian stood by him, net at the ready. As soon as the

fish was close enough, he slid the net underneath and hoisted it into the shallows. Michael dashed into the water to remove the hook, then he knelt down and stared, entranced, as the fish fought to break free of the net. He did not move, even when it gave a great slap of its tail and spattered him with spray and wet sand.

'He's a fine, big fish,' said Ian, holding the rim of the net well above the water. 'What do you want to do with him?'

'Hang on a minute.' Michael hurried over to the bucket and emptied the flappie out without even looking at it. The flappie darted away through the shallows, graceful as a swallow, but Michael did not watch it go. He was busy refilling the bucket with fresh water.

Carefully he lifted the cod from the net. It was cold to the touch and he could feel its muscles bunch and move under the slippery skin. He lowered it into the bucket where it curled awkwardly, too big to straighten out.

'What a fish!' said David.

'That was brilliant, Michael!' said Alice.

'Well done,' said Ian quietly.

Michael said nothing, only stared intently into the bucket, taking in every detail of the fish. The belly was silvery, shot through with colours when the light caught it, and the back was mottled with brown camouflage spots. The flat, golden eye shifted back and forth, hard, cold and fearless.

'Ugly old thing, isn't it?' said Frankie.

Old. Michael thought of the fossil fish he had seen

in a museum. This fish could have been that fossil. It was one of a species that had survived, unchanged, for millions of years.

'Want me to kill it for you?' asked Ian. 'That one's big enough to be worth cooking.'

Michael shook his head. 'No.'

Gently, he lifted the fish from the bucket and lowered it back into the shallows. The fish rested in his cupped hands for a moment then, slowly, with a lazy flick of its tail, it moved off. Michael watched it glinting like gold under the surface of the water until it vanished under an incoming wave.

He brushed his hands off and straightened up, looking around at the others. They were all staring dreamily after the fish, caught in the moment.

'You know what?' said Michael.

'What?' said David.

'I want to do that all over again.'

'Food first,' said Ian firmly. 'It's well past tea-time.'

He produced drinks, sandwiches and fruit from the cardboard box and they settled down to eat. David sat back and took a proper look around the little cove that had once been the main harbour for the town. It was set to one side of the river mouth, where erosion had taken a bite out of the cliffs. On the seaward side, the curve of the cliff protected the cove, and it was shielded from the flow of the river by the wall of the new harbour. On the land side, the cove snuggled in beneath the old town walls, which provided an impressive wind break.

'I don't get it,' said David as he looked around the cove.

'So what's new?' murmured Frankie, lying back on the sand.

Alice laughed and then choked as the mouthful of drink she had been swallowing doubled back and came down her nose. That set Michael off and they leaned their heads together, giggling. David ignored them.

'I mean, look at this place. It's a perfect harbour. Why did they stop using it, Mr Elliot?'

Ian Elliot gave David a sharp look, then he pulled his cap down low over his eyes so that his face was in shadow. 'Oh, you know,' he said vaguely. 'Times change.'

'What do you mean?' asked David.

Ian shifted uncomfortably and stared out to sea. 'Well, for one thing, the river dumps all her silt off to the side here, which makes the way into this place too shallow for the bigger boats.'

'Yes, but it's strange that no one uses it,' persisted David. 'The smaller boats could moor here. The local fishing boats.'

'No. They couldn't,' said Ian, firmly.

'But they could –'

'No.' Ian's face was closed and hard, like the rock he was leaning against. 'They don't like it here.'

David stuck out his chin and ploughed on. 'Why not? It's so sheltered and peaceful.'

'Not always. Some nights –' Ian stopped abruptly and stuffed a sandwich into his mouth.

'What's different at night?' asked David. 'What? Is it the tides?'

'That's it. The tides.' Ian Elliot took another bite of sandwich, picked up his newspaper and opened it with a decisive snap. David looked a question at Alice, who shrugged. Michael kept his head down, drawing in the sand with his finger.

A sudden skitter of pebbles on the rocks behind them broke the silence. They all turned, ready to glare at whoever was climbing down from the harbour wall to trespass in their cove. When they saw the figure in the smart grey suit, Alice, David and Frankie all whirled round to see what Michael would do. A look of panic crossed his face. He dropped his half-eaten apple into the sand and scrambled to his feet.

'Dad . . . ?' he whispered. 'Oh, no! What's the time?'

They all searched their pockets for watches as Mr Adams picked his way down the rocks towards them.

'Time! Time!' hissed Michael.

'The time is six o'clock, Michael,' said Mr Adams, stepping from the lowest rock into the cove.

'I – I'm sorry, Dad. I lost track.'

'Evidently,' said Mr Adams, shaking the sand from his shiny black shoes.

'I'm Ian Elliot,' said Ian, holding out his big hand. Mr Adams gave it the briefest of touches, then bent to brush down his suit trousers. Ian frowned, then tried again. 'Did the boy have to be somewhere, Mr Adams?'

Michael's dad tightened his tie knot. 'Yes, Mr Elliot. He had to be home. At three. Two hours of homework before tea every day is the aim these holidays.'

'Oh, dear. Well you know how it is, on a spring day like today,' said Ian. Mr Adams raised one eyebrow to suggest that no, he did not know how it was, but Ian plunged on. 'Michael here has discovered fishing. I expect he got a bit carried away.'

'Yes, Dad,' said Michael. 'It's really great! I landed ever such a big fish. Can I show you how I've learned to cast?'

'Good idea. In fact, why don't you let your dad have a go as well?' asked Ian. He picked up one of the rods and held it out to Michael's father. 'The boy can teach you how,' he said.

Mr Adams gave Ian a smile without the slightest hint of warmth in it. 'No. Thank you. Fishing would seem to be rather . . .' He stopped and looked Michael up and down, from his dirt-streaked face to his soaked, sand-crusted jeans. '. . . rather messy,' he finished.

'He – he wore his old clothes, Mr Adams,' said Alice.

'Just as well,' said Michael's dad, turning his icy smile on her. 'Because that will never come out.' He jabbed his finger at the stains on Michael's sweatshirt.

'What is this?' cried Frankie, unable to keep quiet any longer. 'A washing powder ad? Sure it'll come out. It's only fish muck!'

'Michael, get your things,' said Mr Adams, ignoring Frankie.

'Oh but, Dad, I want to stay and fish some more! Can't I stay, please, Mr Elliot?'

Mr Adams raised his eyebrows at Ian and waited. Ian's face turned brick red as he stared back at Mr Adams. 'If your dad wants you to go home, then you must go,' he growled. 'It's not up to me.'

'See, Michael? Mr Elliot has had enough of you.'

Ian shook his head. 'I didn't say that. Michael can come fishing with me any time he likes. He's a good fisherman.'

Michael straightened his shoulders and blushed with pride.

'I see. Then the choice is yours, Michael.' Mr Adams waited patiently, certain that Michael would give in, the way he always did.

Michael took a deep breath. 'Thanks, Dad. I think I will stay, just a bit longer. I'll do my homework as soon as I get back.'

Surprise flickered across Mr Adams' face and was gone, replaced by his cold smile. He gave Ian Elliot one sharp nod, then turned and walked off.

'I've got a feeling I've just made an enemy,' muttered Ian Elliot under his breath, when Mr Adams was out of sight over the harbour wall.

'Way to go, Mikey!' cried Frankie. 'What a creep!'

'Frankie! Don't talk about Michael's father like that,' said Ian, without much conviction. 'You wouldn't like anyone to call your dad a creep.'

'That's because he isn't a creep,' retorted Frankie.

Michael turned away abruptly, climbed up the rocks and sat on the top of the harbour wall.

'He's in for it now,' sighed Alice.

Ian scowled so fiercely, his eyebrows met over the bridge of his nose. 'You don't mean Mr Adams will hit him?' he growled.

'No. His dad never touches him,' said David. 'But . . .' He stopped, unable to explain the hold Mr Adams had over Michael.

'Mr Adams is a – a mind bully,' said Alice, grimly. 'He doesn't need to hit Michael to make him feel rotten.'

'It looks like he's gone off the idea of fishing, anyway,' said David, staring up at Michael.

'Come on,' said Frankie. 'Let's go join him.'

Ian Elliot stayed in the cove, packing up the rods and swilling out the bait bucket, while David, Alice and Frankie climbed up to the top of the wall. They sat on the sun-warmed stone beside Michael, who hunched his shoulders, waiting for them to insult his dad. But the insults never came. Frankie handed round sticks of gum and they sat in companionable silence, watching the fishermen unload their catch on to the quayside.

'Are they the ones who gave you the bait this morning?' asked David.

Michael studied the group more closely as they stood around the small pile of fish boxes, shaking their heads. 'No. Why?'

David shrugged. 'I just wondered why they keep looking at us.' As he spoke, one of the fishermen turned his head and stared up at them again. 'Especially him,' added David. 'Are you sure it wasn't them this morning?'

Michael frowned at the staring fisherman and

hesitated. There was something familiar about his dark red hair and the set of his shoulders. Then he remembered. 'I'm sure it wasn't them,' he said. 'The ones I saw this morning told me they wouldn't be back until after dark.'

Suddenly, the red-haired fisherman plunged his hand into one of the fish boxes and came up holding a big dark-blue lobster. He looked up at the children again and beckoned them down from the wall.

'Look at that thing!' yelled Frankie, jumping to her feet. Quickly, she swarmed down the harbour wall on to the quayside. 'Are you coming?' she shouted up to them, then ran off to join the fishermen without waiting for an answer.

'Do we have a choice?' sighed David, clambering down after Frankie.

Alice lowered herself part way down the wall and hung there, braced on her forearms, looking up at Michael. 'Are you staying here?' she asked.

'We-ell,' Michael screwed up his face. 'I don't usually talk to strange lobsters –'

Alice gave a shout of laughter and fell off the wall. She was still giggling when Michael pulled her to her feet and dragged her along the quayside to join the others.

The lobster was easily a foot long. It was making an angry creaking noise and snapping its massive, gun-metal blue pincers.

'I thought lobsters were red,' said Alice.

'Only after they've been boiled,' explained David.

Frankie reached out and touched the whip-like antennae. 'Can I hold it?' she asked.

'Best not,' said the fisherman. 'Those claws could snip off your finger, no bother.'

David was halfway through a cynical chuckle when the man held up his left hand. His little finger ended abruptly just above the knuckle; the skin covering the stump was shiny and pink, like the skin of a pork sausage. David stopped laughing and stared with horrified fascination.

'Eeeuuww!' Frankie jerked her hand away from the lobster and put it behind her back.

'Are you going to boil it?' asked Alice, eyeing the lobster.

'Not mine to boil,' said the man. 'I don't catch lobsters, I use nets. I catch fish. I was working the fishing grounds near Devil's Hole last night.'

'Oh, Devil's Hole!' cried Frankie. 'We were out there yesterday morning.'

The man showed no surprise. 'Were you now?' he said.

'Yeah. My dad works for Trident Oil. We went out on the survey boat.'

Frankie turned to point to *Discovery* further along the quayside so she missed the glance the fishermen shared, but Michael, always the watcher, saw everything.

'Oh yes?' said the man. 'Was there anything – unusual – out there?'

'What sort of unusual?' asked Michael warily, nudging Frankie in the back.

Frankie ignored him. 'You bet there was!' she said. 'That Devil's Hole is one weird place.' She launched into a story of fog, St Elmo's fire and unexplained equipment failure. The fishermen listened intently, especially when she got to the bit about the strange blob on the radar screen. Pleased with the attention she was getting, Frankie began to exaggerate. The shapeless blob became a sea monster with a long neck and flippers.

'Come on, Frankie,' interrupted David disapprovingly. 'There can't have been flippers. It was a radar image, not a photograph. Besides, you didn't even see it – did she, Alice?'

'I don't think so,' muttered Alice, watching Michael's anxious face.

'Is your dad planning to go out there again?' asked the fisherman.

Frankie's face clouded. 'Yeah, he is. He has to. The company want him to do a seismic survey. That's where you set off these underwater explosions –'

'Frankie,' hissed Michael. 'Isn't that confidential oil company stuff?'

'– and then you measure how the sound waves bounce back from the sea bed . . .' Frankie came to a stop, finally noticing how grim the fishermen looked.

'The Collector won't like that,' said the fisherman, and the group shifted uneasily.

'The Collector?' asked David, but no one answered him.

'Sound's like they've disturbed her already,' said a voice from the back of the group.

'They're to blame,' said another man. 'Them and their fancy boat.'

'To blame? For what?' asked Frankie in a small voice.

'For the worst catch we've come home with in a long time,' growled the first man, kicking the fish boxes at his feet. Suddenly, he dumped the lobster back into the box and strode away from the group in the direction of *Discovery*.

'Where are you going?' asked Frankie.

'To have a talk with your dad.'

'You can't!' cried Frankie, running to catch up with him. 'My dad's working. He's trying to figure out what happened to the equipment yesterday. No one's allowed to disturb him while he's working.'

'Looks like he's taking a break,' said the man, pointing to *Discovery*'s fore-deck. Mr Madigan was standing there, stretching and rubbing the back of his neck.

Frankie took off, sprinting towards her father as he waved and hurried off the boat to meet her on the quayside.

'Dad!' she gabbled, slamming into him. 'He lost his finger and there's this lobster and they didn't catch any fish. They think we scared the fish –'

'OK. Shush, I'll sort it out,' murmured Mr Madigan as David, Alice and Michael arrived with the group of fishermen close behind. 'Hi, kids,' he said calmly. 'Had a good day?'

'Yes,' said David, watching the fishermen out of the corner of his eye.

'Glad to hear someone had a good day,' said the red-haired man, stepping forward. 'We didn't.'

'I'm John Madigan,' smiled Frankie's dad. 'I'm sorry to hear you had a bad day, Mr . . . ?'

'Elliot,' said the man. 'Alexander Elliot.'

'But his friends call him Sandy,' said Ian, behind them. David turned and gasped, suddenly understanding why the man seemed so familiar. He was a younger, smaller version of Ian Elliot.

'He's your brother!' cried Alice.

'That's right. How did it go, Sandy?' asked Ian, putting down the fishing rods and draping an arm across his brother's shoulders.

'Bad. Very bad,' said Sandy, still looking at Mr Madigan.

'Ah, well,' sighed Ian. 'That's the fishing for you. One night, nets full to bursting – the next night, empty for no reason at all. No reason at all, am I right?'

Sandy kicked at a stone with his big sea boot and shrugged.

'No reason at all,' continued Ian. 'Mind of their own, those fish. My good friend John here would agree with that. He's done his share of fishing. Have you told Sandy here about your big game fishing, John?'

'Not yet,' said Mr Madigan. 'We were just getting acquainted. Pleased to meet you, Sandy.' He held out his hand and, reluctantly, Sandy Elliot shook it.

'What was all that about?' said Mr Madigan through his smile, as the fishermen walked back to their boats, casting glances over their shoulders at *Discovery*.

'They don't like you surveying Devil's Hole, Dad. They think you might be driving the fish away.'

'And you didn't exactly help back there, Frankie,'

60

said David. 'Exaggerating everything that happened yesterday.'

'I was not!' Frankie stopped and rubbed her nose. 'Yeah, OK, I was. Sorry, Dad. I got carried away. I should've taken notice of Michael. He knew something was up, didn't you, Mikey?'

Michael ducked his head and smiled.

'He's good at that, picking up what's going on,' said Alice. 'That's when I got scared, when I saw Michael's face.'

'So, they want us to stop the survey?' asked Mr Madigan.

Ian shrugged. 'They were looking for something to blame for their bad luck, that's all. Fishermen are very superstitious. It goes with the job. Give them a day or so. They'll calm down.'

''Fraid we can't do that,' said Mr Madigan. 'The equipment all checks out, and the company's waiting for our survey. So. Let's get going.'

5

The harbour was different at night. Quieter. Even the water moved differently. Instead of busy, choppy little waves smacking against the quayside wall, there were smooth silent swells which rose to touch the toes of Frankie's boots before falling away again. Frankie kicked her heels against the stonework and stared down at the empty space where *Discovery* had been moored. Michael was quiet too. He was holding the fishing rod Ian Elliot had left for him and moodily spinning the reel handle back and forth.

'Are you ready for home yet?' asked Alice, watching another tear roll down Frankie's smeared and sticky cheek. 'My mum'll let us watch a video in bed, I expect. And popcorn and crisps and stuff . . .' Alice tailed off as the tear dropped from Frankie's chin and landed on her jacket. It shimmered there for a few seconds, silvery in the moonlight.

'I'm not leaving,' muttered Frankie mutinously.

'But you've been here for hours!' wailed Alice.

'I'm not leaving till they get back!'

'Be reasonable,' said David. 'You can't stay here all night on your own.'

'I won't be on my own.' Frankie jerked her head in the direction of the fishing boats. There was a light on in the wheelhouse of Sandy Elliot's boat. Faint crackles, murmurs and radio static drifted across the still water from the open wheelhouse door.

'See?' said Frankie. 'We're waiting together. Me and Sandy.'

David tried again. 'Your dad said you were to sleep at Alice's house –'

'I don't care what he said!' snapped Frankie. 'He doesn't care about me! He wouldn't've gone out there if he did.'

'He'll be fine,' said David.

'Shut up, Davey! You don't know that! You don't know what's out there. No one does . . .'

Suddenly, Frankie's head came up. She wiped her face on her sleeve, scrambled to her feet and stared up at Fisherman's Row.

'What is it?' asked Alice.

'I know how we can find out what's out there,' said Frankie quietly.

Michael gave her a wary look. 'How?'

'I just remembered something Ian said the other day, in Grandma Elliot's cottage. He said, if you look in the mirror when a fetch appears, you can see what the fetch is trying to warn you about.'

'So?' said David.

'So it's nearly the time when Robert is supposed to appear.'

'So?' repeated David.

Frankie sighed. 'So let's go find out,' she said, heading for the steps.

David grabbed her by the arm. 'Oh no you

don't!' he said, with an edge of panic to his voice. 'That's breaking and entering –'

'No it's not,' retorted Frankie, pulling her arm out of his grip. 'All the windows are open at the back, so we wouldn't be breaking anything. Besides, we're friends of the family.'

Frankie climbed the first few steps, then turned to stare at David, Alice and Michael. 'Are you coming or not? Tell you what, Alice. If you come with me now, I'll come home with you afterwards. Deal?'

Alice hesitated, then sprinted up the steps to join Frankie.

Up they went. Two determined figures, moving further and further away from Michael and David who hovered uncertainly at the bottom of the steps.

'They're not going to stop,' said Michael. 'We can't let them go on their own . . .' He took off after Frankie and Alice, then realised David was not with him. 'Come on, David!'

David stared up at Michael. His face was white in the moonlight. 'I don't believe in ghosts,' he said tightly.

'Then you won't see anything, will you?' said Michael, turning his back and hurrying after the girls.

'And if I do?' whispered David. 'What happens to me then?' He looked over to his bike, still chained to the bench on the quayside. He took the padlock key from his pocket and frowned down at it.

'David?' Alice's voice drifted down from the cliffside. David sighed, pocketed the key and began to climb the steps.

* * *

It was completely dark in Grandma Elliot's back yard. The cliff towered behind them and the cottage blocked the moonlight from the harbour. The cold, dank smell was everywhere. It was as though they were standing at the bottom of a well.

'I wish we had a torch,' whispered Alice.

David smacked a hand against his forehead. 'What was I thinking about this morning, forgetting that? Sandwiches, raincoat, torch for breaking and entering –'

'Shut up, Davey,' hissed Frankie, feeling her way along the wall to the windowsill. 'OK. Got it. Give me a lift up.'

'No need,' said David. 'If we wait a few minutes, Robert'll walk through the yard and open the back door for us.'

'Come on, Michael,' whispered Alice. 'You get the other side.'

Between them, they boosted Frankie up through the open window, while David stood in the middle of the yard with his arms folded. Frankie kicked her legs once, tipped over the window frame and slid down until her hands gripped the inside sill. Carefully, she turned sideways and eased her legs through, one at a time, until she was crouched on the sill like a cat.

Silently, Frankie jumped down to the floor and moved across the wet carpet towards the door, waving her arms in front of her as she went. She started out quite confidently but, as the darkness closed in around her and the chill of the room touched her skin, she began to falter. Where was that door? Her breath began to flutter in her throat and she came to a stop.

A sudden scrabbling behind her made Frankie spin round, arms flailing.

'What's the matter?' whispered Alice, sticking her head through the window.

'You scared me!'

'Sorry.'

'I can't find the door.'

'You must be nearly there,' whispered Alice. 'Just turn round and keep walking. Only a few more steps . . .'

Frankie took a deep breath and set off again. Almost immediately, her hand found the wooden door jamb, then the light switch. With a sigh of relief, she turned on the light and looked back over her shoulder, blinking in the sudden brightness. There was Grandma Elliot's armchair. There were the pipe and the tobacco tin on the mantelpiece with the mirror above. Frankie nodded and went to open the back door.

Minutes later, they were all in the room, clustered around Grandma Elliot's armchair and staring at the door.

'Maybe we should turn the light off?' said Alice doubtfully.

'No, leave it on,' whispered Michael with a tremor in his voice.

'That's right, Michael,' mocked David. 'Very sensible. I mean, how are you going to see him if you turn the light off? Wait a minute though. Maybe he'll glow in the dark. What do you think?'

Frankie turned on David. 'What's with you? Why are you getting at Michael all the time?'

'Because I'm sick of his stupid, super-sensitive act, pretending to – to sense things that aren't there.'

'Well, hey, if you feel like that, I don't want you here.'

'Fine,' said David. 'I'm going home. Don't call me when you get arrested –'

'Look,' breathed Alice.

Frankie and Michael both turned to face the door. David stayed where he was, watching their eyes widen.

'It's him,' gasped Michael.

Nothing there, thought David. Please, don't let anything be there. He made himself turn around.

A man was moving silently across the room towards them. His hair was flattened to his skull and slimed with weed. Water streamed from his beard, weighed down his dark blue jersey and slopped from the tops of his leather seaman's boots with every step he took.

'That's – not possible,' gasped David, gripping Michael by the shoulder.

'His skin . . . Oh, his skin!' hissed Alice, staring in horror at the pure white face. The texture looked soft and spongy, like the bread on their bird table after rain. Alice had the dreadful thought that if she touched his skin, her finger would sink right into it. Or right through it.

'Robert Elliot . . . ?' said Frankie, but the fetch was silent, showing no sign of having heard her.

The apparition moved closer. Every step seemed to take a great effort. They crowded together, waiting, hardly daring to breathe. Finally, he reached the chair, stopped and lifted his head.

'No . . .' whimpered Michael, shaking his head as Robert's sad gaze rested on them. His eyes had no pupils or whites. The whole of each eyeball was black, without a glimmer of light. He stared at them for a long time, then he turned to the mantelpiece and reached out for his tobacco and pipe.

'Now!' hissed Frankie. She jumped out to stand behind Robert and rose up on her tiptoes, staring into the mirror above the mantelpiece. Robert lifted his head and met her gaze in the mirror. Frankie gasped as a picture began to form.

'I can see something!'

David stayed where he was. Michael and Alice joined Frankie, watching as the scene in the mirror took shape. A boat. A flat calm sea. Mist all around.

'It's Devil's Hole,' said Alice.

As they watched, the water around the boat became agitated, as though something big were thrashing about just below the surface. Huge bubbles began to burst all around the boat. Two figures appeared on deck, running to the rails to look over. The boat began to buck and rock, listing to one side as the disturbance in the water grew worse. The two figures fought their way across the deck and back inside.

'The boiling sea! He's showing us what happened to him,' said Michael.

Slowly, Robert shook his head. His dark eyes stared into the mirror and the picture changed, moving closer and closer to the side of the boat until the name showed up clearly.

Discovery.

'No!' cried Frankie.

The scene changed again. This time it showed the window of *Discovery*'s control room, and looking out of it were Ian Elliot and John Madigan. Their frightened faces stared out of the mirror.

'It's happening now!' cried Frankie. 'What are we going to do!'

'It's not happening,' yelled David. 'None of this is happening!' He picked up the pipe and tobacco tin and threw them at Robert as hard as he could. The pipe hit the far wall and broke into two pieces. The tobacco tin rolled and rattled across the floor and came to rest against the skirting board.

Robert was gone. They looked into the mirror and saw their own faces staring back at them. Then the silence in the room was broken as a claxon wailed in the harbour below.

'What's that?' moaned Frankie.

'It's a warning,' said Michael. 'It means they're going to launch the lifeboat.'

They ran out through the kitchen of Grandma Elliot's cottage, slamming the door behind them. As they reached the front lane, a harsh grating noise floated across the still water from the other side of the harbour. The noise was coming from the lifeboat house, which stood poised over the water on black wooden stilts. As they watched, the doors above the slipway at the front of the boathouse slowly opened. Cars and bicycles were pulling up at the lifeboat house and there was even a figure on foot, running along the quayside.

'The crew's arriving,' cried Michael.

The shouts and activity around the boathouse intensified as the bows of the lifeboat emerged at the top of the slipway. The craft edged further out, teetered at the top of the slipway, then tipped forward. With a rattle of chains it shot down the slipway and arrowed into the water, sending up two huge fans of spray. The lifeboat bobbed up to the surface again, water streaming from its flanks. Engines coughed into life and the boat turned, heading for the harbour mouth.

Frankie began to cry.

'It could be a practice,' said Alice, without much conviction.

'At this time of night?' sobbed Frankie.

'Come on,' said David, in charge again now that he had real things to deal with. 'We'll go and talk to Sandy. He'll know what's happening. He had his radio on.'

Sandy was in the wheelhouse, at his radio. When he saw them he came out on deck and gazed at Frankie with an expression of such gentleness and sorrow that Alice felt her mouth turn dry.

Frankie straightened her shoulders and stared back at Sandy. 'I know what you're going to say. The lifeboat. It's not an exercise, is it?'

Sandy shook his head. 'It's a proper call-out.'

Frankie put a hand to her mouth.

'What's happened?' gasped Alice.

'It's *Discovery*. They sent out a distress call. From Devil's Hole. They said something about the water boiling . . .'

'My dad,' choked Frankie. 'Oh, my dad!'

'What else did they say?' asked Alice.

Sandy was silent.

'Please tell us,' pleaded Alice. 'What else?'

'Nothing else,' said Sandy, stiffly. 'They lost radio contact. I'd better get back inside. If I don't hear anything soon, I'm putting out.' He turned and went back into the wheelhouse.

'The Collector,' quavered Michael, imagining a long neck lunging out of the sea and a massive head, the jaws stretched wide, smashing into *Discovery*.

'Shut up, Michael,' snapped David. 'You're not helping.'

Frankie reached out and gripped David by the arm. 'What am I going to do?'

'This way,' said David, coaxing her towards the bench and sitting her down. 'We can wait for news here. Sandy'll let us know what's happening.'

'What news?' said Frankie, dully. 'There won't be any news. They've gone.'

'You don't know that! Look, I'm sure they'll come out of this. Ian knows what he's doing. He got us out of there last time, didn't he?'

'That's right,' said Frankie, nodding vigorously. 'But,' her face collapsed into tears again, 'but, the boiling water . . .'

'I'm sure we'll hear from them soon,' said David.

The minutes dragged by without any news. Frankie jumped at every crackle of Sandy's radio. After a while, she began to shiver. The other three gathered around her protectively.

'How am I going to tell my mom?'

'You won't have to do that, Frankie,' said David.

'Yes I will. There's no one else to do it. I'm all on my own over here.'

'I mean you won't have to do it because your dad'll be back,' said David firmly.

'He certainly will!' said a voice behind them. They turned to see Sandy standing on the deck of his boat with a broad smile on his face.

'Your father is safe and well,' said Sandy.

'He is?' Frankie jumped up. 'He is!' She gave a laugh, which turned into a sigh as her legs folded under her. David and Alice caught her under the arms and lowered her to the bench.

'That's it. Head between the knees,' said Sandy, hurrying over to them with a wet cloth. 'Here, use this.'

Frankie gave a muffled yell as Alice slapped the wet cloth on to the back of her neck. 'Get off me!' she shouted, pushing them all away and sitting up. 'Enough!' she grinned. 'I'm OK!'

'What about Mr Elliot?' asked Michael quietly.

'He's only the hero of the hour,' said Sandy proudly. 'Something happened in Devil's Hole, I don't know what, but they nearly sank. He got them out of it, though.'

Michael's eyes shone and he nodded happily.

'*Discovery*'s well away from Devil's Hole now,' continued Sandy, 'and back in radio contact. The lifeboat's going to meet them and escort them home to harbour.'

'When will they be back?' asked Frankie.

'Oh, not until early morning.' He looked at his watch and frowned. 'So, I suggest you four get home to bed now, before your parents come looking. See you in the morning.'

6

There was a holiday atmosphere on the quayside the next morning. The story of Ian Elliot beating Devil's Hole had got around fast, becoming more elaborate with each telling. Frankie, David, Alice and Michael found themselves being welcomed by Sandy and the group of fishermen who had been so unfriendly the day before.

'But aren't you angry with them for going out there again?' asked Frankie.

'Aye, well. That was the last time,' said Sandy. 'Your dad's been writing his report for Trident Oil on the voyage home. He's telling them it's too dangerous to investigate.'

'Yay!' yelled Frankie, grinning with relief.

'What about my Ian, though?' laughed Sandy. 'He won! That's paid them back for Grandad Robert!'

'Them?' asked Michael. 'What do you mean, them?'

The fishermen exchanged glances.

'Well,' said Sandy, 'what's the harm now? It'll pass the time while we're waiting. "Them", young man, is whatever is out there in Devil's Hole. There are a few theories. UFOs, for instance.'

David blinked. 'UFOs?' he said, trying to keep his voice neutral.

Sandy laughed so loudly, it made everyone jump. 'I know!' he hooted. 'It's one of those theories that makes a lot more sense on a dark night after a few whiskies.'

'Don't tell me. They've had a close encounter with some little green men,' giggled Frankie.

'What, the UFO lot? No. But quite a few folk have seen a green light in the sky over Devil's Hole. And the equipment failure you had the other day has happened to other vessels, too – even to low-flying planes. The UFO believers reckon that some time in the past, a massive alien craft crashed into the sea, causing an impact crater in the sea bed.'

'Devil's Hole,' whispered Michael.

Sandy nodded. 'They think the alien craft might still be down there, trapped and disabled, but partly active. They think this UFO is what causes all the strange lights and the interference.'

'When do they think this – thing – crashed?' asked Alice.

'A long time ago. That place isn't called Devil's Hole for nothing and it's had that name for centuries – as far back as records go. So, we must be talking little grey men with very long beards, by now.'

Frankie laughed again, but the laughter was hesitant this time, with a nervous edge to it. Michael rubbed at his eyes, but could not erase the image of a dull grey shape with a smooth curved edge, jutting from a crater at the bottom of Devil's Hole. He imagined the deep-sea darkness broken by a flickering glow, as veins of lightning pulsed across the surface of the alien craft.

'Wow, UFOs,' said Frankie, glancing over her shoulder at the sea. 'Crazy, huh?'

'So,' said Alice, after a short silence. 'Any other theories? What about this Collector you were talking about?'

Sandy looked down at his boots, then out to sea. 'The Collector. That makes the most sense to me. You see, my grandad wasn't the only one who saw the sea boiling. Over the years, quite a few folk have come back from Devil's Hole with the same story. There are some who think there might be . . . well, they think there might be something big down there, disturbing the water.'

'Disturbing . . . ?' said Alice.

'Yes. Thrashing about.'

'We're talking sea monsters, right?' said Frankie. 'OK. I'm sorry, but if you want us to buy that, you'll have to come up with more than bubbly water. Has anyone ever seen this monster?'

Sandy hesitated and looked at Michael. 'What do you think, son?' he said. 'Has anyone ever seen it?'

The feeling of dread, which had been building in Michael ever since the Collector was mentioned, grew stronger. He stared at Sandy, his eyes wide with anxiety. 'You mean the blob? The blob I saw on the radar?'

'This is crazy,' said David.

'But you said it was the size of a ship!' cried Frankie, staring at Michael. 'That is one big monster.'

'It wasn't a monster,' said David.

'It was coming straight for us,' breathed Alice. 'If we hadn't got out of there so quickly, it might have caught us.'

David folded his arms and scowled. 'I said, it wasn't a monster.'

'Hang on a minute, what happened to the boiling water everyone talks about?' asked Frankie. 'There was no sign of that, was there? It was dead calm.'

'Yeah, well maybe we were lucky,' said Alice. 'Maybe Michael there gave us an early warning with the radar. Maybe if we'd hung around any longer we'd have seen the bubbling water and then it would've been too late to get away from the monster –'

'Hey! Hello there!' yelled David. 'I said, it wasn't a monster!'

'What was it, then?' asked Michael in a shaking voice.

David glared at Michael. 'Now listen to me. You don't know how to read a radar screen. You couldn't know what you were seeing.'

'It was a green blob, the same size as the container ship,' said Michael stubbornly.

'OK. Then it must have been the equipment malfunctioning because of all the interference. The screen flicked on for a few seconds and gave you a false picture. Remember, the blob was gone when we left Devil's Hole.'

'But it could have dived –'

'And that's another thing!' yelled David. 'No creature could move between the depths of Devil's Hole and the surface as though it was riding an elevator!

The change in pressure would kill it. Sandy, come on. You can't really believe . . .'

Sandy shrugged. 'It makes more sense than UFOs.'

'What!'

'Son. I can't pretend there's nothing out there, however much you want me to. Something caused all those boats to be lost. Something killed my grandfather.'

'Right,' said David, grimly. 'I've heard enough. I'm going for a walk.'

He set off along the quayside, walking fast. When Alice appeared at his side he walked even faster, but she kept up easily, matching her stride to his.

'That Michael,' he growled after a while.

'What about him?'

'I've just about had enough of him. Scared of his own shadow. Seeing stuff that isn't there . . .'

'Robert was there, wasn't he? You saw him, didn't you?'

David swerved over to the harbour master's hut and began to study the faded harbour rules and the rabies poster stuck in the window. 'I don't want to talk about that,' he said.

'OK,' agreed Alice mildly.

Just then, the door of the hut swung open, narrowly missing David. He jumped back and they both stared at the man standing in the doorway. He was quite ordinary in every way except that he had the biggest belly they had ever seen. It ballooned out in front of him, overhanging the waist of his navy trousers and straining tautly against his blue harbour master's sweater.

'Good morning!' said the man.

'Good . . .' David stumbled to a halt, unable to take his eyes away from the quivering blue sphere in front of his face. As they watched, it began to wobble, then shake, then judder alarmingly. David stepped back as a rumbling sound built up.

The harbour master was laughing. He slapped his hands against the huge belly and David flinched.

'Don't worry,' laughed the man. 'It won't burst! It only looks as though it might.'

David flushed with embarrassment. 'I wasn't looking at your – at your . . .'

'Belly?'

'Your front,' said David, hearing Alice starting to snigger behind him.

'It's a belly!' roared the man. 'A beer belly. I'm known for it. Know what my grandchildren call me?'

'No,' said David, faintly.

'Jelly belly!'

'Really,' said David politely, as a snort escaped from Alice.

'But you can call me George. Now, what can I do for you?' he said, hooking a chair out of the little office and propping it against the sunny wall of the hut.

David hesitated. Here was a rational man. A man in a uniform. An official. Surely he would be able to talk sensibly about Devil's Hole?

'Mr – um – George, have you heard of –' David hesitated. 'Have you heard of the Collector?'

'Ha! You've been talking to that lot, have you?'

79

David shrugged, smiled and relaxed. 'What lot would that be?'

'The ones who believe there's a sea monster living in Devil's Hole. They call her the Collector.'

'Why?' asked Alice.

'Because she collects boats, drowned men, souls if you like . . .'

'But it's rubbish, isn't it?' said David.

George frowned. 'I can see how these stories grow, though. It's a dangerous job, the fishing. Every time they go out, there's a chance they won't come back. Superstitions tend to sprout in situations like that. For instance –' George pointed to the sky – 'see those gulls?'

'Yes.'

'Do you know why a fisherman would never harm a gull?'

'No.'

'Because they're supposed to carry the souls of drowned men. A fisherman would never kill a sea bird like that, in case his boat became plagued by ship ghosts.'

David smiled tolerantly, then settled down on the warm stones of the quayside. 'What do you think, George? About Devil's Hole?'

George sat back in his chair. 'It does have more than its fair share of drownings and sinkings. That's a fact. The worst incident happened back in the eighteen eighties. We had a much bigger fishing fleet back then, all sailing boats. They went out to the fishing grounds around Devil's Hole one bright, calm day, and a storm came up out of nowhere. No warning at all. Only half the fleet came back. Twenty boats were lost in Devil's Hole.' George shook his head. 'Six crew members to each boat, usually all from the same family. You can imagine what that storm did to the town. There were dreadful scenes in the old harbour that night. Women and children wailing and crying when they realised their menfolk weren't coming home.'

David sat up straight, suddenly remembering Ian's reluctance to talk about the old harbour. 'Is that why they don't use it any more?'

George rubbed his belly and thought about his answer. 'Sort of. Partly,' he said, finally.

'You mean there's another reason?'

'Well . . . there's a bit of a myth grown up around the place. They say that on some nights, you can hear the women wailing and see their paraffin lamps bobbing about just where the top of the old harbour wall would be if it were still standing.'

'Spooky!' shuddered Alice.

'The thing is, the fishermen believe it's an omen of a drowning to come. They don't like that, you see. They don't want to know that, so they keep away from the place.'

'But if Devil's Hole is so treacherous, why doesn't everyone know about it?' asked Alice. 'Why isn't it marked on charts as a danger to shipping or something?'

George rubbed his chin and lapsed into silence. Messages between vessels squawked and crackled on the radio in the office behind him, but he took no notice of them. 'I think that's because Devil's Hole is an out-of-the-way spot,' he said slowly. 'It's not in the major shipping lanes. The only boats to go near it belong to local fishermen, and they don't need any warnings about the place. They know all about it from their fathers and grandfathers.'

Suddenly, a cheer sounded from the other end of the quayside. 'Here they come,' said George, standing up and heading into his hut. 'Clear off now, you two. I've got work to do.'

Frankie cried when her father jumped from *Discovery* to the quayside and caught her up in his arms. She clung to him like a limpet, burying her face in his shoulder. He was laughing as he held her, but the tears dripped from his chin into her springy black hair, where they caught and sparkled like crystals.

Watching them, Alice felt her own eyes fill with tears. Beside her, David was gruffly clearing his throat but Michael was smiling as he looked up at Ian Elliot.

'I'm glad you're back safe,' he said.

'Me too, son,' said Ian tiredly. 'I thought we'd had it. I thought we'd chanced our luck at Devil's Hole once too often.'

'Don't you dare go out there again,' said Frankie fiercely, when the crowd had finally dispersed.

'I won't,' promised Mr Madigan. 'I wrote my report to the company on the voyage home. I've told them that Devil's Hole is unsuitable for drilling.'

'So there's no oil down there?' asked David.

'Actually, I think there is. But there's also a problem.'

'Did the survey show something up, then?' asked David.

Mr Madigan shook his head ruefully. 'Yet again, we didn't manage to do a survey. We made a good start,' he added, moving over to the quayside bench. 'Then things started to go wrong, didn't they, Ian?' He lowered himself on to the bench and Frankie flung herself into his lap.

'What happened?' asked Michael, looking at Ian.

Ian sat down beside Mr Madigan. 'It was strange. I thought we were in luck to start with. Devil's Hole was behaving itself. No fog. No interference. We started the sweeps for the survey. It's called mowing the lawn, because you cover the area in strips, back and forth, back and forth. We'd only done two sweeps when it happened, just like it did with my grandad.'

Ian paused and wiped his hand across his face.

'The boiling water?' whispered Alice. Ian nodded.

'The thing is,' said Mr Madigan, 'I think I know what causes it.'

'Is it a sea monster?' said Michael, looking at him with wide eyes.

'I think there's a much more logical explanation,' said Mr Madigan. 'And I'm no radar expert, but this might even explain your blob, Michael. Like I said, I think there is oil down there. Oil and gas. My guess is there's an anticline at the bottom of Devil's Hole. That's a sort of dome of rock, with oil or gas trapped underneath. Now, I think there's a weak spot in the dome – a fissure or a crack of some sort. Pressure builds up to a certain point, then the whole thing shifts and releases a huge bubble of gas –'

'Of course!' interrupted David. 'The gas bubble shoots up to the surface –'

'– and makes the water look as if it's boiling,' finished Alice.

Mr Madigan nodded. 'That's why the boats sink. The skin, the surface of the sea, breaks up so much, there's nothing to hold them up. That's what happened to us today. *Discovery* started to sink. It was terrifying.' Mr Madigan shuddered and Frankie wrapped her arms around his neck. 'If it wasn't for Ian, we'd be at the bottom of Devil's Hole now.'

'Get away! I just got lucky,' smiled Ian.

'More than luck,' said Mr Madigan. 'Tell them what you did.'

'Well, I remembered how you're supposed to get out of quicksand. You don't move fast. You take it slowly – the smaller the disturbance, the better. That's what I did. Instead of trying to blast out of there with the engines at full throttle, I just sort of eased her out of it.'

'He was really cool! We were getting lower in the water all the time, but he kept plodding on towards calmer water and – here we are!'

Ian looked sad. 'When I think of my grandad, and all those other boats . . . Ah, well. It's over now.'

'It will be over,' said Mr Madigan, pulling a large brown envelope from the inside pocket of his jacket. 'As soon as I get home and fax this report to Trident Oil.' He tipped Frankie off his knee and stood up.

'Oh, let's not break it up yet, Dad,' pleaded

Frankie, looking round at the others. They all nodded in agreement. They had come through an experience which no one else had shared and there was a closeness between them they did not want to lose.

Mr Madigan hesitated. 'Well, I should get this off . . .'

'You could use George's fax machine,' said Ian, pointing to the harbour master's hut. 'He'll charge you an arm and a leg, mind, but then we could all go along to the old harbour afterwards and get a bit of fishing in. It's a lovely day, what better way to spend it?'

'OK,' smiled Mr Madigan.

'Come on, guys!' yelled Frankie. 'Follow me to the harbour master's hut!'

'There,' said Mr Madigan a few minutes later as he fed the last sheet of paper through George's fax machine. 'Now it's over.'

They had reached the wall which separated the old and new harbours when they heard the shout. 'John! John Madigan!'

'It's George,' said David, pointing to the harbour master standing in the doorway of his hut.

'I wonder what he wants?' muttered Ian. As though in answer, the harbour master waved a sheet of paper above his head. 'Fax!' he yelled.

Mr Madigan sighed. 'Nearly made it,' he said, glancing up at the harbour wall they had been about to climb. 'Frankie, honey, do me a favour –'

'I know, I know,' grumbled Frankie, jogging off to collect the fax message.

'What do you think it is?' asked Alice.

'It'll be a reply from Aberdeen, questions about the report. Whatever they want to know, it can wait until tomorrow.'

'Here. George says you can pay him for this one on the way back,' panted Frankie as she skidded to a halt in front of her father and held out the fax message.

'Doesn't miss a trick, does he?' laughed Mr Madigan, waving to George. He took the paper and read the message. 'What?' he gasped, scanning the page a second time.

'Problems?' asked Ian.

'Jarvis,' said Mr Madigan.

Ian laid down his rod and net and put his hands on his hips.

'Who's Jarvis?' asked Michael, looking up at Ian Elliot's stony expression.

'Jarvis is a big wheel in the company,' said Mr Madigan. 'He's involved in the search for new oil fields. Some would say he's very successful at his job.'

'Ha!' exploded Ian. 'Others would say he's a menace. It's oil at any cost, as far as Jarvis is concerned. I know. I've worked with him before.'

Frankie looked up at her father's grim face and swallowed. 'What's the message, Dad?'

'"Survey incomplete,"' read Mr Madigan. '"Report unsatisfactory. My ETA is nineteen hundred hours."'

'ETA?' asked Alice.

'Estimated time of arrival,' said David. 'He'll be here this evening.'

7

The bright green company helicopter hovered over the harbour, searching for a landing space. Its searchlight picked out the flat clifftop above Grandma Elliot's cottage and it swerved in for a landing. The little group on the quayside in front of *Discovery* watched in silence as two men clambered out of the helicopter and ran, crouching, across the flattened grass until they were clear of the rotor blades. With a dip of its nose and a high-pitched whine, the helicopter rose into the pale evening sky and headed back up the coast.

'Uh-oh,' said Mr Madigan. 'Looks like he's planning to stick around for a while.'

'Which one's Mr Jarvis?' asked Alice, as the two men started to descend the steps that led from the cliff top, past Grandma Elliot's cottage and down into the harbour.

'The one in front,' said Ian. 'I don't know the other one. John?'

Mr Madigan squinted through the dusk and shook his head. 'No. Never seen him before.'

'The one in front looks like a weasel,' snarled Frankie as Mr Jarvis stepped on to the quayside. Alice sniggered. Mr Jarvis did look very much like

87

a weasel. He was sleek and slim. His nose and chin drew his narrow face to a point. His beady black eyes darted from side to side, missing nothing.

'Be nice,' murmured Mr Madigan. 'Let's find out what he wants first.'

Frankie glared at the man as he approached, but her glare was wasted. Mr Jarvis did not even glance at the children. He stopped in front of Mr Madigan.

'Mr Jarvis!' said John Madigan, stepping forward. 'How was your trip? Have you got somewhere to stay?'

Mr Jarvis waved his hand impatiently. 'You say there is oil,' he snapped, holding out the report.

Mr Madigan blinked. 'Uh . . . I said I thought there *might* be oil, but we couldn't complete the survey. It's a dangerous place, Devil's Hole. Unstable. Any oil down there is not worth the risk –'

'Wrong,' said Mr Jarvis flatly. 'It's our job to keep our clients supplied with fuel, to keep our rigs busy and our men in work. Oil is always worth the risk.'

'Whose risk?' growled Ian.

'Not yours,' snapped Mr Jarvis. 'Not any more. I'm taking you off this survey.'

Mr Madigan gasped. 'Now hold on a minute –'

Again Mr Jarvis waved his hand impatiently. 'Can't you see what's been going on here, Madigan?'

'What do you mean?'

'Elliot's a local man.'

'Yes?'

'So he's got local loyalties. His brother's a fisher-man and I happen to know that the fishermen here don't want their livelihood disturbed. They don't want us exploring Devil's Hole in case the fish get frightened away.'

'How do you know about that?' gasped David.

Mr Jarvis glanced down at the children for the first time. 'Move on,' he ordered. 'This is a business meeting.'

'Yeah, and it's our business!' retorted Frankie.

Mr Jarvis ignored Frankie and turned back to her father. 'He took you in, Madigan. Elliot and his mates took you in. UFOs, sea monsters ... You've been tricked.'

'I must object,' said Mr Madigan. 'My recommendations are grounded in science, not stories –'

'Jarvis.' Ian's voice was dangerously soft.

Mr Jarvis turned to face him. 'Are you still here? I told you, you're off this survey. Bradley is taking over from you. He's a pilot I can trust.'

The man behind Mr Jarvis smiled nervously but no one took any notice of him. They were all watching Ian Elliot's furious face.

'Trust? John Madigan knows he can trust me,' grated Ian.

'That's right. I trust him absolutely.' Mr Madigan took a deep breath. 'I must tell you I shall refuse to cooperate with his removal. I wouldn't be here now if it wasn't for Ian.'

'Ah, the heroic rescue today. Obviously the possibility of sabotage never crossed your mind, Madigan,' said Mr Jarvis.

'What!' Ian's voice was full of outrage. He stepped forward and towered over Mr Jarvis. 'Are you saying

I deliberately damaged the equipment on *Discovery*? I hope you've got proof to back that up.'

Mr Jarvis stepped back and a tremor of doubt crossed his face. 'Let's just say I don't want you on board that vessel again. Any personal items will be forwarded to you – Ow!'

Mr Jarvis doubled up and clutched at his shin.

'You shut up!' cried Michael, clenching his fists. 'Just shut up and don't say anything else about Mr Elliot, or I'll kick you again!'

Alice put both hands over her mouth and David frowned nervously, but Frankie gave Michael an admiring look. 'Hey, Mikey!' she grinned. 'With you all the way!'

'Look out!' cried David as Mr Jarvis lunged for Michael.

'You little –'

'I mean it!' cried Michael, dancing backwards out of his reach. 'I'm not afraid of you! I'll kick you harder next –'

'Michael!'

'Dad?' Michael twisted round and stared up into his father's face, his eyes wide with shock.

'Apologise to this man immediately, Michael.'

'No! I won't! He's trying to sack Mr Elliot!'

Mr Adams raised his eyebrows at Mr Jarvis. 'You are Ian Elliot's superior?' he asked.

'That's right,' winced Mr Jarvis, rubbing his leg.

'Good.' Mr Adams smiled coldly at Ian. 'Then I wish to lodge a complaint. My name is Adams. Mr Elliot has been encouraging my son Michael to run wild in the harbour this week.'

'Dad!'

'Michael won't come home when he is told –'

'I forgot –'

'I have to come and fetch him, and his clothes –'

'That does not concern me,' began Mr Jarvis.

'Oh, but it does,' said Mr Adams. 'Mr Elliot put my son and three other children in danger earlier this week. He put them in danger by taking them out on a Trident Oil vessel. They were on board *Discovery* during the first attempt to survey Devil's Hole.'

There was a silence. Mr Jarvis stepped closer to Ian and Mr Madigan, staring up into their faces. They shifted uncomfortably. They were both big men but suddenly, he seemed to be the one with all the power.

'Look, it was my decision to take them out,' said Mr Madigan. 'It was nothing to do with Ian.'

'Thank you, Mr Adams,' said Mr Jarvis, still staring at Ian and Mr Madigan. 'I agree, this is a serious matter. Unofficial passengers, no insurance cover, putting children in danger. If Head Office got to hear of this –'

'All right,' growled Ian. 'You don't need to say any more. I'm going.'

'Wait a minute,' said Mr Madigan.

'John, he's got us over a barrel. Take on the new pilot. Do what he tells you.'

Mr Madigan looked at his friend and spread his arms wide. Ian gave a quick nod and turned abruptly, walking away along the quayside.

'Hey, come on!' said Frankie. She pointed at Mr

Adams. 'You shouldn't take any notice of him! He's just jealous because Michael likes Ian better than him –'

'Shut up, Frankie,' hissed David.

Alice sidled up to Michael and linked her arm through his. He kept his head down, making it difficult for her to read his expression in the deepening dusk, but she could feel his chest shaking with suppressed sobs.

'Good,' said Mr Jarvis. 'Madigan. A quick inspection of *Discovery* now, please.'

'Then what?' said Frankie's dad, watching Ian walk away.

'Then we'll take her out tomorrow morning.'

'I am not going back to Devil's Hole,' said Mr Madigan.

'Just a few miles out tomorrow,' said Mr Jarvis smoothly. 'A trial run to test all the equipment and let Bradley here get used to her.'

'Very well, Mr Jarvis,' said John Madigan with icy politeness. 'Follow me.'

'We shall go too, Michael,' said Mr Adams. 'You have stayed out well past your allowed playtime as it is.'

Michael shook off Alice's hand and turned to his father. 'I hate you!' he yelled. 'You spoil everything! Go away!'

Mr Adams put out a hand towards his son but Michael took off, sprinting down the quayside and scrambling over the wall into the old harbour.

Alice, David and Frankie stared at Mr Adams without a word as he straightened his tie, looked down at his feet, and finally walked stiffly away in the direction of town. They could hear his black shoes clicking on the concrete long after his grey suit had faded into the darkness.

'Phew!' David shook the tension out of his shoulders and looked at the other two. 'What do we do now?'

'Go after Michael,' said Alice.

David looked unsure. 'I think he wants to be on his own,' he said.

'Yeah, probably, but he's going to get us anyway,' said Frankie.

They found Michael down in the shadows under the harbour wall. He was sitting so still and quiet they nearly missed him, but Alice spotted the luminous stripe on his trainers.

'Here he is,' she called softly to the other two. Michael drew his knees up to his chest as they moved around him, looking for rocks to sit on, but he said nothing.

They waited, watching the colour drain from the sky and listening to the gulls fluttering down to roost all around them. The waves hissed in and sighed away again. At last Michael sat up and turned to Alice. 'Can I stay at your house tonight?' he asked.

'Sure,' said Alice. 'If you can stand sharing a room with the twins.'

'Your mum won't mind?'

'You know she won't. She never minds – as long as you let your dad know where you are.'

'Thanks,' sighed Michael and lapsed into silence again.

'Stars are getting brighter,' said Frankie. 'Look at that one over there.'

'That's not a star,' said David. 'It's too low. And it's moving.'

They all looked at the yellow light as it hung low over the water.

'What is that?' asked Alice. The gulls rustled their wings on the harbour wall above her head. Another yellow light appeared, closer this time, bobbing back and forth in the little cove.

'Over there,' whispered Frankie, pointing out two more lights moving across the sand.

'And there,' said David. 'Five, six, eight of them . . . more!'

The lights were suddenly everywhere, bobbing in mid-air above the water and the sand and the tumbled rocks of the old harbour wall.

'Maybe we should leave?' said Frankie.

'Why?' asked David.

'I – I'm not sure.'

'You don't think . . .' Michael's voice quavered. 'You don't think they're UFOs, from Devil's Hole?'

David gave a snort of disgust. Behind them the rustling of feathers grew louder. Alice glanced up and gasped.

'Look,' she breathed.

There were gulls edging the harbour wall from end to end, packed together so tightly there was not a single break in the line. Their eyes were like a row of black beads, each one with a yellow light reflected in its centre.

'Whoah!' yelped Frankie, jumping to her feet.

'Shhh!' hissed Michael, easing himself off the stone to stand by Frankie as the gulls moved restlessly. 'Don't startle them.'

Alice and David both stood up with slow, careful movements. The birds shifted. Their webbed feet paddled the harbour wall, making tiny slapping noises. Their sharp beaks speared the air.

'I told you we should leave,' moaned Frankie. 'Let's get out of here.'

'How?' whispered Alice, pointing up at the gulls blocking their way.

Frankie covered her head with her hands. 'I hate birds.'

'There's more of them on the beach,' said Michael. 'Look, rows and rows of them. What's going on?'

David shook his head. 'It's not natural behaviour. They should be squabbling. Fighting for their patch.'

'There are more lights,' said Alice. 'Up on the clifftop too. I think Frankie's right. We should leave –'

Alice stopped as a sound began to grow in the little cove, rising and falling like the waves. It was a sound full of pain and deep, deep sorrow. Alice listened and felt fear draw a bristling line from the base of her spine to the top of her head.

'Make it stop!' cried Frankie, blocking her ears as the wailing grew louder.

'Is it the birds?' asked Michael.

'No, it sounds like crying,' said Alice, backing up against the harbour wall. 'Like people crying – but there's no one here.'

95

They huddled together as more and more lights appeared, bobbing and dipping in mid-air. The gulls stood like sentries, watching, and the wailing echoed around the cove. Alice began to cry softly. David looked about, wildly, trying to find an explanation. His heart slammed and jumped inside his chest.

Suddenly Alice reached out and gripped David by the arm, digging her fingers into the muscle. 'Gulls!' she cried. 'Souls! And the wailing – remember?'

'What? Tell me,' demanded Frankie as David yanked his arm out of Alice's grip.

'It's just a story,' snapped David. 'George told us gulls carry the souls of drowned fishermen. And he said this place was haunted by the widows of drowned fishermen, carrying their paraffin lamps and waiting for the boats to come back.'

'Oh, please let's go,' cried Michael. 'Let's go!'

'It's just a story!' yelled David, as the wailing grew louder. 'It's not real!'

'It's an omen of a drowning to come,' said Alice. 'George said.'

Michael curled against the harbour wall. 'I don't like this. This feels bad –'

'I've had enough of you!' shouted David. 'It's amazing. Everyone says how clever you are but, really, you have no sense at all, do you?'

'Davey!' said Frankie, giving him a shocked look.

David threw up his arms and the gulls on the wall above him danced away, then back, sending a tremble of movement down the whole line. 'Well, I'm sick of the whole spooky business. It's nonsense, the lot of it and he –' David stabbed a finger at Michael, 'he swallows it all. Look at you, Michael! Jumping at your own shadow!'

'Stop it, David,' said Alice. 'Leave him alone.'

'Evidence, Michael. Where's the evidence? Think about all those museums you've dragged us round. Think about your precious fossils and your precious dinosaur bones. Don't they tell you anything? They're real, Michael! They're real and they've left their mark behind, not like stupid sea monsters and – and ghosts with fairy lights and –'

Michael blinked. 'Hang on,' he said. 'Say that again . . .'

But David turned away. 'I'm sick of stories and legends. There's an explanation for everything. There is. There is!'

Still shouting, David took off, running across the sand towards the lights.

'There is! There is!' he yelled, running at the silent ranks of gulls and forcing them into the air in an explosion of feathers.

'David!' shrieked Alice. 'Come back!'

But David was halfway across the cove, running and shouting and flailing his arms as a storm of gulls wheeled and flapped around him.

Alice started running too, desperate to stop him from reaching the lights. 'Don't –' she gasped, stumbling and falling and scrambling up again with the salty grit of sand in her eyes and mouth. 'Don't . . . You don't know what those lights are . . . !'

'There is an explanation! There is!' yelled David, far ahead of her now. 'There is!'

David hit the lights and Alice fell to her knees. The

wailing stopped, cut off as though a soundproof door had slammed shut. The lights flared up then winked out, leaving the cove in total darkness. Everywhere the gulls rose, squawking and fighting and wheeling above the old harbour, then fanning out and away over the starlit sea.

Alice stood up. 'David,' she called, her voice loud in the sudden silence. 'David?'

Wiping the sand from her eyes, Alice stared at the spot where she had last seen him.

'David?' called Michael, coming to a stop beside Alice.

'David?' echoed Frankie from the harbour wall. There was no answer. David had gone.

They ran along the beach, searching the dips and hollows, peering behind rocks. Alice stared at the patch of sand where he had disappeared, trying to see footprints, but white moonlight and black shadow made it hard to pick out any shapes.

They reached the end of the little bay and started again, moving back the other way in case they had missed something the first time. The bay was empty.

'It can't be!' wept Alice. 'He's got to be here somewhere. Maybe he passed out . . .'

Michael turned to stare out at the waves as they rolled into the shelter of the old harbour. 'Maybe he's in the water . . .'

The three of them waded in up to their thighs, then turned and worked their way back to shore, each quartering their own section of the bay. They dipped their arms down into the water, feeling for

anything that could be a body, and they called and
called. They searched until their arms and legs ached
so fiercely with the cold, they were all crying. One by
one, they gave up and waded back to the beach.

'Do you think they took him?' asked Frankie, as
they stood together, shivering.

'Who?' asked Alice, still gazing around the bay.

'The ghosts. The ghosts of the widows.'

Alice turned and began to run awkwardly towards
the harbour wall, her wet jeans clinging to her
legs. 'We need to get some help,' she gasped. 'We
should've done that to start with.'

'Wait,' said Michael.

Alice turned to look at him, blinking away her
tears. He was staring up at the roof of Grandma
Elliot's cottage.

'Look.' The roof of the cottage was lit up by the
moon. The chimney stack rose above the roof and
smoke was pouring from the stack.

'I know where he is,' said Michael.

8

'I lit the fire for Robert,' said David. 'Grandma Elliot said he always went to the fire to warm himself when he came home. There was some coal and kindling in the bunker in the yard.'

'It's a great fire, Davey,' sniffed Frankie, standing as close as she dared and watching the steam curl from the sleeves of her jacket. 'Seems almost cosy in here now. And the smell's not nearly so bad.'

'I mended his pipe too,' said David. He pointed to the mantelpiece. The pipe and tobacco tin were back in place. 'I found some glue, in the drawer there.'

'I can't even see where it was broken,' said Alice, nodding approvingly.

David smiled. 'Thanks.'

'How did you get here, Davey?' asked Frankie. 'I mean without us seeing you leave the old harbour?'

'I climbed the cliff,' said David. He remembered the nightmarish scrambling, grasping for ledges that crumbled away, clinging to clumps of springy grass while his feet scrabbled for a hold.

'That was dangerous,' said Alice gently.

'I know. At the time, though, it was easier than coming back to face you. I – told Robert I was sorry, when he appeared. I want to say sorry to you too, Michael.'

Michael beamed up at David from the fireplace kerb where he was sitting. The firelight danced across his face, hiding the blush which reddened his cheeks. 'No need.'

'Yes, there is. I've been the stupid one here. I got scared, because there were things I couldn't explain. I knew, you see.'

'Knew what?' asked Michael.

David hesitated. 'I – knew Robert was real. I knew all along. When I stood in here on my own, I could *feel* how sad he was, you know?'

Michael nodded. 'I know.'

David sighed. 'I knew he was real, but I couldn't explain it. And that scared me. So I took it out on you. All that stuff I said in the old harbour – I didn't mean it.'

'I've been thinking . . . about what you said.'

'I told you,' interrupted David. 'I didn't mean it –'

'No,' said Michael. 'Not that bit. You talked about the fossils and the dinosaurs. And I think I've worked out what Devil's Hole is.'

'Hey! Way to go, Michael!' said Frankie, turning around to steam her bottom dry.

'It was when David said dinosaurs,' explained Michael. 'Even then, in the old harbour, when I was busy being upset, there was this ping.'

'Ping?' said Alice.

Michael nodded. 'Yes. This connection in my head. Ping! A connection between dinosaurs and Devil's Hole.'

101

'Go on,' said David.

'OK. The dinosaurs died out about sixty-five million years ago –'

'I knew that,' said Frankie.

'But the big question is, why did they die out? Have you heard of catastrophe theory?'

'Sounds like my brothers,' giggled Alice.

'No, it's this theory that the dinosaurs died out all of a sudden because of a catastrophe, a big disaster.'

'Definitely my brothers.'

Michael tutted impatiently. 'Will you be serious?'

'Sorry. What was the disaster?'

'Well, some people believe there was this massive asteroid bombardment sixty-five million years ago.'

'How do they know?' asked Frankie.

'First of all there are these big craters all over the world which they think were caused by asteroid impacts. And, they've taken soil samples from that time which show up lots of metals like iridium which – and this is the killer – you don't get on earth.'

Michael smiled triumphantly but the other three looked blank.

'In other words,' explained Michael, 'they're from space. They're meteorite metals. They prove there was a bombardment. And there was something else in these soil samples. Lots of soot left from the forest fires which broke out everywhere after the asteroids hit.'

David jumped up, suddenly realising what Michael was getting at. 'Devil's Hole is an asteroid crater!' he said excitedly.

'I think so,' said Michael. 'Why else would there

be such a deep hole in a shallow sea?' He shook his head and stared into space, his eyes dreamy and distant. 'It must have been a massive asteroid. It got through earth's magnetic field and it didn't burn up in the atmosphere. Massive. It must have been, to make such a deep crater. And Mr Madigan's right, it is unstable down there. The impact would have caused cracks and fault lines – not a place to start drilling for oil.'

'Wow!' Alice closed her eyes and pictured a huge ball of flame with a molten red tail streaming behind it. She saw it getting bigger and bigger, filling the sky as it screamed down towards the ground. She shuddered as she imagined the fires, the earthquakes and the storms which must have followed.

'Do you think it's still down there?' she asked, opening her eyes again.

'Most of it would have been blown to bits when it hit, but my guess is the metallic core is still down there. That's what's causing all the interference.'

'How would it do that?' asked David.

'Imagine. If it's a metal we've never come across before and it's giving off some sort of strong magnetic force, it could mess up navigational equipment, make compasses spin, even interfere with radio signals.'

'And cause the sea frets and the St Elmo's fire,' added Alice.

Michael looked doubtful. 'You mean a sort of magnetic fog?'

'Maybe. And remember, Frankie's dad said St Elmo's fire was electro-thingummy.'

'–static. Electrostatic,' said Frankie.

'Right. And isn't that all to do with magnetism?' Michael shrugged. 'You could be right.'

'Well, anyway,' said David, 'it all makes a lot more sense than sea monsters or UFOs.'

'Exactly,' beamed Michael. 'And it means Mr Madigan can give horrible Jarvis and the oil company a good reason for leaving Devil's Hole alone.'

'Yeah!' crowed Frankie. 'I can't wait to tell him! I mean, I can't wait for Michael to tell him. Let's go!'

Alice looked doubtful. 'We can't let him see us like this,' she said. 'In fact, we can't let any of our parents see us like this. They'd throw a fit. What are we going to do?'

'I know,' said Frankie. 'We'll go back to my place. It's nearest the harbour and there's no one there. You can all call your various parents from there and tell them you're staying the night. I'll shove all the clothes in the washing machine, tumble dry them . . . No one'll be any the wiser!'

'So, what now?' asked Alice the next morning as she watched David finish off his fourth slice of toast.

'We go down to the harbour and wait for Mr Madigan to get back from the trial run,' said Michael. 'I can't wait to tell him!'

'If he'll still speak to you after what your dad did,' said Frankie. 'I – I mean . . . I didn't mean that, Michael.'

'It's OK. That's what's so good about this. It'll make up for my dad. Do you see?'

Alice nodded. 'Come on, then. Let's get down there.'

There were three people sitting on the quayside bench when they arrived at the harbour.

'That's Ian, Sandy and Grandma Elliot,' said Alice, quickening her pace. 'Come on, Michael.'

Michael held back, worried that Ian might blame him for what his father had done the night before. But the big man was welcoming and friendly, moving over to make room for him on the bench. Michael settled down in the sun with a relieved smile on his face.

'Well, tell them, then!' exploded Alice, unable to wait any longer.

'Tell us what?' said Grandma Elliot.

'I'm not sure,' said Michael shyly. 'But I think I know what's wrong with Devil's Hole.'

Michael launched into the meteorite theory again.

'See? Told you he was clever,' said David, when Michael had finished.

Michael smiled and turned to Ian. 'What do you think?' he asked.

'Makes sense to me,' said Ian carefully, glancing at Grandma Elliot. 'What about you, Gran?'

Grandma Elliot shook her head and sighed. 'You can dress it up anyway you like. Monsters, UFOs, meteorites – they're all just ways of saying Devil's Hole is bad. Evil. If it's easier for you to talk about meteorites than to believe the warnings from my man and the souls in the cove, then that's fine by me. I'm not going to argue with you as long as you keep away from the place.'

'You won't catch me near there,' muttered Sandy.

'And I've got no choice,' growled Ian.

'This'll get my dad off the hook, too, I reckon,' said Frankie. 'When will they be back, Ian?'

Ian glanced at his watch. 'They should have been back by now. They were only going a few kilometres out. Tell you what, let's have a stroll down to the harbour master's office. They'll have left their plans with George.'

'I'll come with you,' said Sandy, stretching as he stood up.

George was bent over the chart table in his little hut. He had abandoned his harbour master's sweater and his shirt strained across his belly as he straightened up to greet them. Frankie gazed at the quivering shirt buttons, waiting for one to pop off and fly across the room.

'Come on, Ian,' George was saying. 'You know they won't be back for ages yet. You can't get out to Devil's Hole and back in a morning.'

A silent tremor of shock ran through the little hut.

'What?' said George, looking at their horrified faces. 'What did I say?'

'They're not going to Devil's Hole,' said Ian.

'Oh yes they are,' said George, hooking a chart from the pile and laying it on the table in front of them. 'That's their chart. That new pilot Bradley lodged this with me this morning. See?'

'But they can't be going there,' said Frankie, her voice high with fear. 'My dad would never have gone out if they were heading for Devil's Hole . . .'

106

Ian leaned over the chart, then slammed his fist down on to it. 'They're going all right,' he growled. 'Jarvis has taken your dad out without telling him where they're really headed.'

'Oh, Ian. My dad! What're we going to do?'

Ian ran his hands through his hair and looked at his brother.

'Come on,' said Sandy. 'My boat.'

The children had trouble keeping up with the two brothers as they stretched their long legs and sprinted along the quayside, but they managed to reach the fishing boat and clamber in as Ian was still untying the lines.

'Oh no you don't,' said Ian. 'You'll have to wait here. Stay with George and we'll keep in radio contact.'

'No,' said Frankie, sitting down on the deck and folding her arms. One by one, the other three joined her.

In the wheelhouse, Sandy fired the engines and the boat began to pull at her moorings.

'Come on!' snapped Ian. 'I haven't got time for this.'

'We're not moving,' said Frankie.

'Then I'll carry you off!' roared Ian.

Michael flinched but Frankie stuck out her chin. 'And while you're dumping one of us on the quayside, the last one you dumped'll be climbing back on board!'

'Look, Trouble. It might be dangerous out there.'

Frankie stared at Ian, her dark eyes big with tears. 'It's my dad, Ian. It's my dad!'

Ian sighed, untied the stern line and jumped on board. He went into the wheelhouse and threw four life jackets out on to the deck.

'Thanks,' sighed Frankie, pulling on the life jacket.

'Just stay out of the way, all of you,' growled Ian, ducking back into the wheelhouse.

Frankie moved to the bows and stayed there, searching for any sign of *Discovery*.

'You won't spot her yet,' said Ian, bringing Frankie a mug of tea. 'We can't catch up with a vessel like *Discovery* in this old boat, not when she's on the move. It's all the way to Devil's Hole, I'm afraid. We've got her right on the edge of the radar screen, but they won't respond to our radio messages.'

'But my dad would answer, wouldn't he?'

Ian shook his head. 'It's my bet Jarvis is in control of the radio. When I get my hands on that –' Ian took a deep breath and smiled down at Frankie. 'So, don't think you've got to stand here like a figurehead. Move around a bit, stretch your legs, go below if you want a rest or something to eat.'

Frankie nodded but stayed where she was, watching the horizon until her eyes hurt from the glitter of sun on water. Finally, she was rewarded.

'I see it!' she yelled. 'I see *Discovery*!'

The others crowded around, watching, as the fishing boat drew nearer to the survey vessel.

'It looks deserted,' said David.

Ian stood beside them, scanning *Discovery* with battered binoculars. 'The decks are empty,' he said. 'But there must be someone in the control room.

She's being held in position right on the edge of Devil's Hole. If thee was no one on board she'd be drifting.'

'At least we reached them in time,' said Frankie happily. 'Before they sailed in there.'

Alice put her arm around Frankie. 'He'll be fine now,' she said. 'We're nearly there.'

Michael stared over the water towards Devil's Hole as Sandy's boat slowly pulled closer to *Discovery*. 'No fog today,' he said. 'It looks just like any other bit of sea, doesn't it?'

'It's what's underneath the surface that's the problem,' said Ian, handing David the binoculars.

David focussed and scanned the decks of *Discovery*. Suddenly he stiffened. 'The submersible's gone!'

'What?' asked Ian.

'That deep sea submersible you showed us. It's gone.'

Ian snatched the binoculars back. 'The crazy idiot's launched it,' he breathed. 'That's why *Discovery*'s still here. He's gone down into Devil's Hole in the sub!'

9

Ian shoved the binoculars back into David's hands and ran for the wheelhouse, shouting at Sandy to hurry.

'Don't worry,' said Michael. 'Mr Madigan won't be in the sub. He wouldn't go near Devil's Hole.'

'So why isn't he answering our radio messages or out on the deck waving to us?' whimpered Frankie. 'He should have spotted us by now.'

The others were silent. Frankie was right – where was he?

Sandy pulled his boat alongside *Discovery* and held her there while Ian threw lines on to *Discovery*'s decks.

'Hold her steady, Sandy!' he shouted, and in the wheelhouse Sandy raised his hand to show he understood. Ian climbed up on to the gunnels of the fishing boat and grabbed *Discovery*'s deck rail. With a practised swing, he vaulted aboard and secured the ropes.

'John?' he cried. 'John Madigan?' There was no reply.

Ian leaned over *Discovery*'s deck rail and looked down at Frankie. 'I'm going to the control room to find out what's happening. You stay there, do you hear?'

Frankie nodded and waited for Ian to disappear from view.

'Right,' she said, 'here goes.' She grasped one of the lines for safety, then climbed up on to the gunnels of the fishing boat and leapt for *Discovery*. She grabbed the rail, hauled herself up on to the deck and disappeared.

'Well, if she can do it . . .' David jumped too, then reached down over the deck rail and helped Alice aboard *Discovery*. Michael hesitated, imagining how it would be if he fell between the boats. Would he be crushed first, or drowned?

'Michael!' hissed David.

Michael took a deep breath, grabbed the line and climbed up on to the gunnels. With his heart beating against his chest, he leapt for *Discovery*'s deck rail and clung on while David reached over his back and hauled him up by the belt of his trousers.

'Come on then,' whispered David.

Michael clambered shakily to his feet. There seemed to be no strength left in his knees as he wobbled slowly towards the control room. He was nearly there when he noticed something on the deck which everyone else had missed as they rushed past. It was lying beside the big steel A-frame which lowered the submersible into the water. Michael frowned and changed direction. His eyes widened with horror as he realised what he had spotted. Slowly, he bent down and picked the thing up.

When he reached the control room, Frankie was crying and Alice was trying to comfort her.

'Mr Madigan's gone down there with Jarvis,' whispered David, glancing at Michael.

Ian was arguing with the pilot. 'How could you let them go down there, man?' he roared. 'You haven't enough crew for a safe submersible launch!'

'Look,' said the pilot, 'you don't argue with Mr Jarvis if you want to keep your job. You of all people should know that!'

'No job is worth putting lives in danger. Turn that monitor back on and re-establish radio contact with the sub. Now!'

The pilot shook his head. 'Mr Jarvis knew you were following us. He told me to turn it off if you came aboard.'

'Why?'

'He thought you might try to . . . cause trouble.'

Ian slapped a hand to his forehead. 'Not the sabotage rubbish again! John knows I would never do that!' He stopped and gave a puzzled frown. 'I can't believe John was stupid enough to go down there. Didn't he object?'

The pilot nodded. 'Oh, yes. He absolutely refused to go. He said he was going to stop Jarvis going too. They had a big argument. Then they went out on deck and the next thing I knew, Mr Jarvis was saying Madigan had changed his mind and I was to go ahead with the launch.'

Ian shook his head. 'I can't believe he decided to go.'

Michael swallowed and cleared his throat. 'Um, I don't think he did decide to go. I think he might

112

have had no choice.' Michael held up his hand. 'I found this out on deck.'

They all stared at the smooth round stone he was holding.

'It's Ian's ballast stone,' said Michael. 'The one from the chart table.'

'Is that . . . is that blood on it?' breathed Alice, pointing.

'I think so,' said Michael.

Frankie covered her face with her hands and swayed on her feet.

Ian turned back to the pilot, who was beginning to look very worried. 'Did you see John Madigan, after they went out on deck?'

'No. I thought –'

'You thought!' roared Ian. 'All right. Think about this. Jarvis has knocked my friend out and then taken him down in that sub without his consent. There are at least two or three criminal charges mixed up in that lot. Do you still want to stick to what Jarvis told you?'

The pilot shook his head.

'Good. So turn that monitor back on and re-establish radio contact.'

The pilot worked quickly and soon a murky underwater picture appeared on the monitor screen, transmitted from a camera fixed to the nose of the submersible. The only illumination came from the sub's powerful searchlight penetrating a metre or so into the gloom. It was trained on the side of the Devil's Hole crater. They all gathered around the monitor, scared of what they might see, yet at the same time, fascinated.

'It's still descending,' muttered David, watching the crater wall rise past the camera lens.

'What are they?' shuddered Alice as a cluster of pale bloodless hands wavered into the light.

'They're called dead men's fingers,' said the pilot. 'It's a sort of soft coral.'

'Forget the nature lesson,' growled Ian. 'Get that radio going.'

The pilot picked up the handset. '*Discovery* to sub.'

The radio crackled. 'Have they gone, Bradley?' came the tinny voice of Mr Jarvis.

The pilot swallowed nervously and pressed in the button on the side of the handset. 'Mr Jarvis, can I speak to Madigan?'

'Answer me. Have the intruders gone?'

Frankie leapt forward and grabbed the handset. 'Dad? Dad, it's me, Frankie. Answer me, please, Dad. Say something.'

There was a long silence, then Mr Jarvis laughed. 'He's got a bit of a headache right now.'

Ian lunged for the handset. 'You listen to me, Jarvis. You need to get out of there. It's dangerous. Start the ascent now, before something terrible happens.'

Mr Jarvis spoke again, and this time he was deadly serious. 'I don't believe you, Elliot, and I'm going to find oil down here whether you like it or not. Over and out.'

There was a click, then silence.

'Jarvis? I know you can still hear me . . . Jarvis?' Ian threw down the handset in disgust.

114

'What now?' asked Frankie.

Ian shrugged. 'I'm sorry, Frankie. There's nothing we can do. Jarvis is in control.'

'Look,' said Alice hastily, as Frankie's face crumpled, 'there's no fog today, no radio interference. It all seems calm and normal. Maybe if they keep to the edge of Devil's Hole, they'll be all right.'

They waited, watching the sub sink deeper and deeper. The numbers of startled fish caught in the searchlight grew fewer, then stopped appearing altogether. The coral and marine plants coating the crater wall thinned out until there was nothing but bare rock. The sub had reached depths too cold and dark to support life.

Increasingly, the group in the control room found themselves looking past the pale circle of the searchlight beam to the swirling darkness beyond. Half-seen shapes seemed to flick across the edge of the monitor screen, gone before they could focus on them.

'What was that?' gasped Michael as something sleek and muscled coiled through the darkness.

'Where?' asked Alice.

'No, it's gone.'

'I think I saw something,' whispered Frankie.

'I think we're imagining things,' said David carefully.

'I hope so,' muttered Alice.

Again and again, Ian tried to talk to Jarvis, but there was no response. Frankie retreated to a chair and huddled there, refusing to talk. The tension grew in the silent room. When a whoop

115

of delight suddenly blasted out of the radio, they all jumped.

'Look at that!' yelled Jarvis. 'It's pouring out! Can you see that, Elliot? Watch.'

Everyone gazed at the screen as the camera on the nose of the sub panned the rock.

'Look!' cried Alice, as the camera stopped. 'It's oil!'

The powerful searchlight had picked out a rock. The rock had a jagged crack running across it and a powerful black stream was pouring steadily out of this fissure, billowing and curling through the water like clouds in a clear sky.

Frankie stood up and gripped the back of the pilot's chair. 'Tell him to come back, now he's found it. Tell him to bring my dad back.'

The pilot turned from the monitor to look at them. 'That's not oil,' he said slowly. 'It's a black smoker.'

'A what?' said Michael.

'The proper name for it is a hydrothermal vent. I've never seen one in this sea before. You usually find them on fault lines, where the earth's crust is unstable.'

David looked at Michael. 'What if this crater had been caused by a meteorite impact?'

'That would explain it, I suppose. You see, if I'm right, that black stuff is water.'

'Water? What's happened to it?' asked David.

'It's water that has seeped down through faults in the earth's crust until it comes within a few hundred metres from a chamber of molten rock. The water gets heated to an incredibly high temperature, then it blasts back out of the rock. If that was happening on the surface, you would have steam many times over, but the pressure is so great down there, it stays as water.'

'Elliot?' crackled Jarvis. 'You're very quiet up there. What's the matter? Do you still not believe I've found oil? Tell you what, I'll move in for you to get a closer look.'

'No!' yelled the pilot into the handset. 'Don't do that, Mr Jarvis. That would be very dangerous.'

'Dangerous? How?'

'It's not oil – it's superheated water. If you take the sub into that, it'll melt the viewports.'

Mr Jarvis laughed. 'Elliot put you up to that, didn't he? Nice try, Elliot, but guess what? I don't believe you.'

The sub turned, moving closer to the billowing black cloud.

'No! Stop him!' shrieked Frankie.

'Mr Jarvis! Turn back! The viewports are perspex. If they melt, that's it, you've had it. Think of the pressure down there!'

The black smoker grew bigger as the camera edged closer.

'Can you see it yet, Elliot?' jeered Mr Jarvis.

'Yes, yes,' said Ian, grabbing the handset. 'I see it. You were right. It's oil. I can see it's oil. Now pull back!'

Blackness filled the whole screen, twisting and curling with muscular strength. There was a groaning, creaking noise from the radio and the start of a scream, then a static hiss filled the control room.

'No!' cried Frankie.

Ian grabbed her and held her close to his chest as the monitor screen went blank.

Alice and David stood frozen to the spot, too shocked to cry. Michael rushed out on to the deck and was sick over the side. He stood in the spring sunshine, looking out over the sparkling blue water, but there was no sign of any wreckage.

Michael rested his forehead on the cool metal of the deck rail. He felt absolutely desolate.

'Here,' said Ian, gently setting Frankie down beside him. 'I think it's best she stays out here while I inform all the authorities. Look after her.'

Frankie was shaking. She clung to the rail and would not let go. Michael had no idea what to say so he stood by her, as close as he could. Alice appeared and stood on Frankie's other side, gently brushing the hair from her face. David slumped against the rail with his hands shoved deep in his pockets.

'It would have been quick,' he said after a while. 'He wouldn't have known a thing about it.' Frankie nodded and gripped the rail harder.

'You can stay with us until things get sorted,' offered Alice.

'Be quiet,' said Frankie.

'Sorry,' said Alice. 'I didn't mean to –'

'No. I meant, listen . . .'

Frankie turned from the rail, her head cocked to one side.

It came again. A muffled thud, then another, from below decks.

'Did you hear that?' Frankie looked at them with a strange, wild excitement on her face.

'Yes, I heard,' said David and the other two nodded.

Thud. Thud.

Frankie gasped and rushed for the door that led below decks.

'Come on,' said David. 'We've got to stay with her.' He raced after Frankie, hurling himself down the stairway to the cabins, with Michael and Alice crowding down behind him.

Thud! Thud! It was much louder now. Frankie ran down the tiny corridor to the cabin where they had slept less than a week earlier.

'The key!' she sang, her face bright with joy. 'The key. It's on the outside!'

'Oh, my –' David's face lit up as he suddenly realised what Frankie had already guessed.

'It's all right,' he yelled, turning to Michael and Alice behind him. 'It's all going to be all right!'

Frankie turned the key and fumbled with the door knob, laughing and sobbing at the same time.

'What is going on?' cried Alice as the door flew open.

'See?' said David.

For a few seconds everything was still. Alice and Michael stared, wide-eyed, at the scene in front of them, then they turned and hugged one another, grinning like clowns. David looked from them to Frankie with a satisfied look on his face, as though he had organised the whole thing himself.

For in the doorway of the cabin stood Mr Madigan, blood still oozing from a gash on the side of his head.

'He locked me in,' he said in a dazed voice. 'Jarvis locked me in.'

'Dad,' breathed Frankie. 'My dad.'

'Hi, honey,' said Mr Madigan. He held out his arms and Frankie walked into them with a contented sigh, like a traveller coming home.

Mr Madigan was wrapped up like a parcel, winched into a yellow rescue helicopter and taken to hospital, protesting that all he needed was a couple of aspirin and a butterfly plaster. Ian turned *Discovery* and headed for home, with Sandy following at a more sedate pace in the fishing boat.

'The doctor says it's just a precaution,' said Frankie happily, staring after the distant dot of the helicopter as it skimmed the sea.

'He's going to be fine,' said David.

Michael gazed out over the stern rail towards Devil's Hole. 'Poor Mr Jarvis,' he said.

Frankie bristled. 'Hey! He was a horrible man.'

'I know. But nobody deserved that,' said Michael. 'And why was he so horrible? Perhaps, if someone had bothered to find out, instead of being scared of him . . .'

'Oh, puh-leeze,' jeered Frankie, but Alice smiled at Michael, understanding that he was thinking about his dad.

'You're right,' she said. 'Everyone deserves a second chance.'

Michael nodded seriously. 'But I'll never be scared of him again, Alice. He's got a lot smaller since I saw what he did in the harbour.'

'You've lost me,' said Frankie.

'Never mind,' said Alice, winking at Michael.

'Fog's coming in,' said David.

Alice looked out over the stern rail. Behind *Discovery*, Sandy's fishing boat chugged steadily through the clear water, under a cloudless blue sky. 'Where?' she asked.

'There,' said David, pointing to the horizon where a grey sea fret shaped like an upturned bowl was forming over one patch of sea.

'Devil's Hole,' breathed Alice, shuddering.

'That is so weird,' said Frankie, staring at the thickening dome of fog.

'I told you,' sighed David. 'There's a perfectly natural explanation for that fog –'

'Yeah, yeah,' interrupted Frankie. 'But I still think it's weird. It is! Some places just are.'

'She's right,' said Alice.

David folded his arms and looked at Michael. 'What about you?'

'I'm with Grandma Elliot,' said Michael. 'We can talk all we like about aliens and monsters and meteorites, but we only really need to know one thing.'

'What?'

'Devil's Hole is a bad place,' said Michael, simply.

'Oh, very scientific,' muttered David.

121

Michael shrugged and turned to stare out over the stern of *Discovery*. Alice joined him, her long black hair whipping over her face in the sea breeze. Frankie pushed and shoved her way in between them and David settled himself on the other side of Alice. Together they watched, in silence, until the grey smudge which was Devil's Hole dipped below the horizon and disappeared.